Melissa,

a *touch* of
CINNAMON

♡
Bethany
Lopez

A Touch of Cinnamon

Copyright 2018 Bethany Lopez

Published January 2018

ISBN—978-1983758485

Cover Design by:

Makeready Designs

Editing by:

Red Road Editing / Kristina Circelli

Proofreading by:

KMS Freelance Editing

Interior Design & Formatting by:

Christine Borgford, Type A Formatting

also by
BETHANY LOPEZ

Young Adult:
Stories about Melissa—series
Ta Ta for Now!
xoxoxo
Ciao
TTYL
With Love
Adios
Nissa: a contemporary fairy tale

New Adult:
Friends & Lovers Trilogy
Make it Last
I Choose You
Trust in Me
Indelible

Contemporary Romance:
A Time for Love Series
What Happened in Vegas (Prequel)
8 Weeks
21 Days
42 Hours
15 Minutes
10 Years
3 Seconds
7 Months
Novella—*For Eternity*—Coming Soon

a *touch* of CINNAMON

a *three sisters catering* novel

BETHANY LOPEZ

To my children, for asking, "Did you write a chapter today?" and "Did you finish your book yet?" Your love and support mean more than I can express. I love you.

Prologue

"No," I said sleepily into the phone.

I'd been up late studying for a quiz, and didn't bother looking at the face of the phone to see who was calling. I just wanted the ringing to stop.

"Tash."

My name on my sister's lips, in that tone, had me sitting up and coming fully awake.

"Millie, what's wrong?" I asked.

"It's Mom . . . Tasha, you know I wouldn't be calling unless it was serious," my oldest sister said, the pain in her voice tearing me apart. "You need to come home."

Tears pricked my eyes as the reality of what she was saying crashed down on me.

Our mother had been downplaying her illness for so long, I'd begun to believe she'd be okay. But, Millie telling me to leave school and come home meant the worst thing imaginable was happening . . . our mother was dying.

"I'm on my way," I stated simply, then pressed end and sat on my bed, staring at nothing as my mind raced.

It's a sign. That's what the voice in my head was telling me. A sign that I was so caught up in Jericho, I'd been losing sight of everything else. My family, my studies, my independence.

I'd left my mother, sisters, and the only home I'd ever known, so that I could find myself and figure out what I wanted to do with my life. Instead, I'd met Jericho, become infatuated in all things Jericho, and had forgotten my real reason for being here.

I'd skipped holidays and birthdays, opting to stay with Jericho instead. Not wanting to leave him even for a short weekend.

And now, my mother and sisters needed me, and I needed to go home.

I packed quickly, grateful for the first time that my dorm room was too small to hold too much stuff, so it didn't take long.

Thirty minutes later, I'd sent an email to my advisor letting her know what was happening, my small car was loaded down with all of my belongings, and I was turning out of my dorm parking lot and headed home.

I kept my eyes straight ahead as I passed Coffee Time, the coffee house where Jericho and I'd had our first date, and where he was probably right then drinking a cup and surfing the internet while he waited for me to meet him.

I knew he'd hate me, but I hoped, eventually, he'd realize that what we'd had was more than either of us could handle, and was bound to burn out soon. And, maybe, one day, he'd forgive me for leaving without saying goodbye.

Because if I'd seen his face, or even heard his voice on the phone, there was no way I'd ever be able to leave.

One

Natasha ~ Present

"**H**ave you heard from Millie yet?"

I looked up from my planner to see my sister Dru coming into the office. She looked nervous, which was weird, because Dru didn't get nervous.

"No, why? Does Claire need help out front?" I asked.

Dru waved her hand and said, "No, she's got everything under control."

I narrowed my eyes, took in the way she was bouncing slightly on the balls of her feet and fisting her hands at her sides. She wasn't *nervous*, nervous, she was *excited*, nervous. Something was going on.

"What is it?" I asked, pushing my chair back and standing. The movement caused my back to twinge, so I placed my hand on my lower back and stretched from side to side. I guess I'd been sitting too long.

"What's what?" Dru asked quickly, *suspiciously*. "Nothing's going on."

"Oh, *something* is going on . . . You know something that I don't and you're going to tell me what it is."

"Or what?" she asked, jutting out her chin and cocking a hip. Now she was trying to deflect her lie by getting feisty. I knew my sister's game all too well.

"*Or*, I'll get suddenly sick on Saturday and you'll have to deal with Mrs. Gunderson, *Mother of the Bride from Hell . . .*"

Dru lost all signs of feistiness and cried, "You wouldn't!"

"You know I would," I taunted. I wasn't bluffing and she knew it.

"But, she made Big Stan at the flower shop cry," Dru protested.

"She makes *everybody* cry. Now, spill. What's happening with Millie? Did something happen in Graceland?"

Dru bit her lip, looked at the clock, then sighed.

"Oh, fine, they'll be back any minute, so I kept my promise to Jackson and didn't spill his secret."

"His secret?" I asked, then my eyes widened and my mouth dropped. "Did he propose at Graceland?"

Dru squealed and nodded, and we clasped hands as we both started jumping up and down.

"Either Kate Spade is having a seventy percent off sale, or someone spilled the beans," I heard Millie say dryly.

Dru and I turned to see her standing in the doorway of the office, her hand out in front of her to show off the ring. We took our jumping and squealing to her and both grabbed her hand at the same time.

"You said yes!" I exclaimed.

"She said yes," Dru mimicked.

"*I said yes!*" Millie cried, and started jumping with us.

"Oh my God, it's beautiful, and so totally you," Dru said as she leaned in to get a bird's eye view of the ring.

"Tell us everything," I urged. "Did he get down on one knee? Recite poetry, or . . . *oh*, more Keats? Was Kayla there? Where did he do it?"

Millie laughed at our exuberance and suggested, "How about we grab some coffee and I'll tell you everything."

"Okay, but let's go down to Rooster's," Dru suggested. "I know you're just getting back, but I could use a change of scenery."

Millie nodded.

We walked through the kitchen, Millie stopping to give Claire a hug and ask how things had been while she was gone.

"She can give you the lowdown on the kitchen later," Dru said impatiently, pulling Millie toward the door. "I only have thirty minutes until my next meeting, and I don't want you skipping any details."

Millie laughed and said, "All right. Claire, I'll come talk to you in a bit."

"Sure thing, Mills, everything's great here. Go catch up with your sisters."

We made it through the kitchen and into the storefront, where Millie had to stop to say hi to a couple other people, then we were finally out on the street in front of Three Sisters Catering.

"Maybe we should have snuck out the back," I said with a laugh, then allowed my eyes to drift across the street, like they always did when I went out the front door, and I stopped dead in my tracks, 'cause he was there.

Standing outside of Prime Beef, the steakhouse he'd opened mere months before we'd opened up shop right across the street, was Jericho Smythe.

The man I'd fallen in instant lust, and almost as immediately in love, with, in accounting class my freshman year of college. The man who'd consumed my thoughts and feelings for over a year after that meeting, and who I'd unceremoniously left without so much as a Dear John letter years ago.

The man who still hadn't spoken to me, but had only glared at me from afar.

The man who still made my heart yearn, my breath quicken, and my knees go weak with just a glance.

I turned my head quickly and grabbed my sisters by the hands, urging them to keep walking toward Rooster's.

"I'm guessing you two didn't talk things out while I was away," Millie said softly, her eyes on Jericho.

I shook my head.

"Well, I'm pretty sure Jackson's going to have him involved in the wedding in some capacity, so you won't always have the luxury of having Main Street between you. You need to swallow your pride and talk to him, Tash. Explain what happened and clear the air so that you can at least be civil to each other."

I smiled sadly and nodded, but stopped myself from correcting her.

It wasn't pride that kept me from talking to Jericho, it was fear. Not fear that he wouldn't understand, and would never forgive me. *But, fear that he would . . .*

Two

Jericho ~ Present

*T*he pain that hit my gut was as instantaneous as the rapid beating of my heart at the sight of her.

It happened every time.

Every. Single. Time.

I did my best to ignore it, to ignore *her*, but I'd been trying that since I'd arrived over a year ago, and it was just as impossible now as it had been then.

Not when I could hear the sexy timbre of her voice, see her gray-blue eyes widen with fear every time they landed on me, or feel the weight of her longing. Because whether she wanted to admit it or not, it was there.

Just as I still longed for her.

I stood a moment longer, watching the three sisters walk down Main Street, Natasha's bright-red bob swaying with each step, then forced myself to turn away and walk inside.

I strolled through Prime Beef, glancing around at my staff and making sure the dining room was ready to open for lunch. I didn't bother going into the kitchen, I knew my head chef, Hector, would have everything under control. That was why I'd hired him, after all, so that I wouldn't have to worry about what was going on in the kitchen.

I was a business major with a hospitality minor, and Hector was a graduate of Le Cordon Bleu with ten years of experience. We made a great team, and although I ultimately owned Prime Beef, I considered him my partner.

Prime Beef wouldn't be what it was without both of us, and I was extremely proud of what we'd accomplished in such a short time.

Still feeling the effects of my Natasha sighting, I headed for my office, pulled open my mini fridge, and grabbed a cold water. I sat at my desk, uncapping the water, and took a long drink, then I leaned back in my chair and closed my eyes.

Out of all the places in the world I could have opened my restaurant, a small town may not seem like the obvious choice. In fact, Hector had tried to talk me out of it a couple times, arguing that we'd fare better in the big city, but I wouldn't budge.

Natasha had talked about this place a few times while we were together, but she'd either downplayed the quaintness of the town, or hadn't been able to see it for what it was at the time. She *had* been hell bent on getting away from her hometown and becoming independent, so maybe she hadn't realized what she had here until she'd gotten older.

Not me. The second I'd walked down Main Street, I'd known there was no place else I'd rather live and work.

Coming from the streets of Philly, I'd known hard, cold, and hungry, but what I hadn't known was beauty, warmth, and community.

It was true, I'd originally come here to find Natasha. To confront her about her cowardice. To rage at her for leaving me without so much as a *goodbye*. To find out why . . . But, I hadn't done any of those things.

Instead, I'd bought a prime piece of real estate on Main Street, informed Hector that I'd found our location, and hired a moving van.

It was a stroke of luck that three months into development, Natasha and her sisters had set up their own business and moved in right across the street. At that time, I'd already been living there for four months, and I still hadn't run into Natasha.

To say she was shocked would be an understatement, and to say seeing her had rocked me to my very core would be completely accurate.

She'd cut and died her hair, and had obviously gotten a few years older, but she still looked exactly the same. My first instinct had been to go to her, to take her into my arms, and tell her how much I'd missed her, but the look of utter horror on her face had stopped me cold.

Yes, she'd left me without looking back, and yes, I'd come here to rail at her for breaking my heart, but never in a million years had I expected to see that look on her face.

My confidence had fled and I'd become uncertain of how to proceed, so I decided to wait. To give her time to come to terms with my being here, and to let her come to me when she was ready.

That had been over a year ago, and she'd never come.

No, instead, she scurried away like a frightened mouse any time she laid eyes on me.

Hell, the one time we'd actually been in the same room together, at a bar with her sisters and our mutual friends, she'd looked at me like I was the offender, and had fled the bar almost in tears.

Her sisters had also looked at me like I was the leaver instead of the leavee, which was totally baffling.

I was the injured party here, not her, so why had they all acted like I was the asshole? And, why did Natasha's eyes widen in fear whenever she saw me. She had to know that no matter how angry with her I was, I'd never harm her in any way.

I opened my eyes and let out a heavy sigh.

I'd been fucking around for over a year, confused, and yes, scared of what finally confronting Natasha would mean. Would she regret leaving me, or was she happy with her decision? Did she still feel anything for me, or had she moved on?

These were the thoughts that kept me up and night, and no matter what the answers, it was time to stop torturing myself.

I was going to finally man up and confront Natasha.

Three

Natasha ~ Past

I moved the strap of my backpack up more securely on my shoulder, then let out a short breath as I fought for the courage to open the door.

I'd only been on campus for three days, and today was the first day of class.

I was terrified, felt completely awkward, and I missed my sisters.

"C'mon, Tash," I muttered, then lifted my hand and pushed.

Voices chattered happily as I entered the lecture hall and glanced up, checking the wall clock to make sure I wasn't late when I saw all the people that were already inside.

Nope, I was five minutes early.

I'd planned to be fifteen minutes early, but I'd spent five outside of the Math Complex, urging myself to enter, and another five in front of the classroom.

Not wanting to bring any sort of attention to myself, I moved to the right and started scooting past the chairs in the back row, with the intention of getting to the middle as quickly as possible, getting everything out of my bag, and sitting before anyone noticed me.

My head was down as I shuffled, my long chestnut hair falling around me, obscuring my face. Which was why I didn't realize anyone else was in the row until large boots came into sight, just as I was tripping over them.

"Oh," a male voice grunted, then I was being steadied by a pair of strong hands. "I've got you."

I looked up, struggling to contain my mortification, then froze as lightning struck me on the spot.

He was tall, so very much taller than me, with dark hair and striking features. His hands on my arms felt like brands, and his eyes seemed to consume me with their intensity.

"You okay?" my dark stranger asked, his voice deep and thrilling to my ears.

"Uh, yeah, sorry," I managed, although I'm not sure how.

I was captivated, mesmerized, staring up at him as he grinned slightly down at me.

He was obviously older, and a lot more confident than I was, and there was something about him that exuded strength. He had a *sureness* about him . . . I wasn't sure how else to explain it.

"Take your seats," I heard ordered from the front of the room, and knew our professor had arrived and was ready to start class.

Yet, I found it almost impossible to move.

Luckily, the deep-voiced man who was still holding me upright was still able to function, and he moved me to the side and turned me, then slid my backpack off of my shoulder and urged me to sit in the seat.

The seat next to his.

I sat with a thud, accepted my backpack, and opened it quickly, avoiding all eye contact with my neighbor as I pulled out my notebook, accounting book, and the bag that held my pens and pencils.

Once I had everything laid out, I shifted in my seat and tried to focus on what the professor was saying. It was extremely difficult though, because I was hyper aware of the long, jean-clad leg that kept brushing innocently against my bare leg.

Sparks flashed with each touch, and I fought to control my breathing and keep my gaze straight as I felt him watching me.

When I didn't give him the attention he sought, although I did notice that the table in front of him was empty, no book, paper, or any sort of writing utensil, my stranger reached in front of me, zipped my pouch open slowly, and took a pen from inside.

I waited, unsure of what he was going to do but desperate to find out, then flinched slightly when his fingers brushed against my wrist as he turned it on the table. I felt the whisper of the pen on my flesh, then glanced down when my wrist was released.

Jericho.

That's what he wrote on my wrist, his name. It felt like he'd written it on my soul, and I swear, I could still feel the heat of his fingers on my flesh.

Tap, tap, tap.

I glanced over to see my pen tapping on the table as he waited.

I gave one last glance at the professor, to make sure we weren't about to be called out for not paying attention, then took the pen from Jericho's hand and reached for his arm.

He turned it for me, so the underside of his forearm was facing up, and I braced myself as my hand made contact with his tanned skin. His forearm was strong, muscular, although not overly so. It was also soft and warm, and I found myself wondering what the rest of him would feel like.

Hoping my hair concealed the blush on my cheeks, I put the tip of the pen to his forearm and wrote, *Natasha.*

Before I could pull away, Jericho captured my hand in his, turned it, and wrote in my palm.

Coffee?

He's asking me out? Is this real life?

I glanced around the room, sure that this was some sort of freshman hazing, where the mysteriously hot upperclassman found a naïve underclassman to mess with. It had to be a joke. Why else would a guy like Jericho be interested in taking a girl like me for coffee?

I'd grown up with my sisters as best friends, our father had left us when we were little, and our mother had raised us. The town I came from was small. So small that we knew we couldn't get away with anything without our mother finding out, so we never tried.

That was part of the reason why I'd left home to go to school. Not just to get out on my own, but to actually *live* a little. To make decisions, good and bad, and to handle the consequences of those decisions on my own.

So, even though I was sure it was a joke, and I knew I might end up getting hurt or humiliated, I took the pen from his hand and wrote, *yes*, on his palm.

I dropped the pen then, turned away, and focused completely on what the professor was saying. I opened my book and took notes, all the time aware of Jericho next to me, and the fact that after class, I was going on my first college date with the hottest guy I'd ever seen.

It took all I had not to squeal out loud, but you can bet your bottom I was screaming on the inside.

It was time to start living.

Four

Jericho ~ Present

I got up early, earlier than most, and although initially it had been because I was working to get my fledgling restaurant up and running, now it was a force of habit.

I'd already gone for a morning run, showered, and dressed for my day, now I needed coffee. I strode through my ranch-style home, glancing out the large, unencumbered windows to enjoy the view of my three acres, like I did each morning. It was a view I loved, and had never thought I'd ever be able to experience.

As a boy, I'd lived with the loud sounds of the city, wandering dirty streets, and learning how to take care of myself, while I fought not to get caught up in a way of life that could ruin any chance I had of ever getting out.

My mom was a junkie, strung out more often than not, and my father . . . a ghost.

When I was sixteen, I'd lived on my own in our one-room apartment. My mother had been serving one of her stints in jail, and I'd found a job working as a busboy in a local kitchen. The pay sucked, but they gave me free food, and let me work around my class schedule.

I'd come home late one night after my shift, eager to get in a shower and finish up my homework, so I could get at least a few hours of sleep. When I saw a strange car parked on our street, I'd thought nothing of it, even though it was obviously expensive. We often had people of means stopping by to buy drugs or score a hooker from our complex, but when I got to my door, I was wary when I found a man in a suit leaning casually against it, his eyes on his phone.

"You lost?" I'd asked, trying to sound tough.

I was already taller than most men half my age, but I wasn't looking for any trouble.

"Jericho Smythe?" the man asked, putting his phone in his pocket and looking me over.

"Who's asking?"

"My name is Barnes, Clive Barnes, and I'm your grandfather's lawyer," the man replied.

"I don't have a grandfather," I said, then moved passed him to the door.

"Well, you did . . ." he said, and I turned to look at him, curiosity getting the better of me.

"Did?" I asked.

"Your father's father, Jerome Smythe, has unfortunately passed away."

"You know my father?" I asked, unable to keep my cool at the possibility of finding out information on the man my mother refused to discuss.

"I did," Mr. Barnes said, his tone cautious.

I didn't notice his tone, however, as excitement coursed through me.

"Does he know about me? Can you tell me where he is?" I asked eagerly, all pretense gone.

"I'm sorry, Mr. Smythe, your father passed away about ten years ago."

All hope fled me as a crushing sadness filled me. It may seem strange, to feel so forlorn over someone you'd never even met, but I'd always held on to the hope that one day my father would come for me, or I'd find him, and I'd be able to escape the life I'd been living.

"Oh," I managed.

"Anyway, Mr. Smythe, what I'm here to tell you is that as your grandfather's only living heir, you've come into a bit of money . . ."

A bit of money had been an understatement, as it turned out. Unwittingly, my father had helped me escape the life I'd been living, at least inadvertently. My mother hadn't made it out of jail that time, instead getting more time added to her sentence, and leaving me to raise myself.

With my inheritance, I'd been able to go away to school and never look back. It had also given me the ability to follow my dreams and open my own restaurant, and to buy my house, on this land.

I didn't take a bit of it for granted, and I was mostly happier than I'd ever been . . . except for that year in college when I'd had Natasha.

Newton, my black cat, ran out in front of me and jumped onto the kitchen counter, eager for breakfast. I'd never been able to have pets growing up, unless you counted the strays that were often in our alley, and although I'd always wanted a dog, my hours with Prime Beef had been insane and I didn't feel right having a dog if I wasn't home to be there for him.

Isaac Newton, on the other hand, was very self-sufficient, and often acted like this was his home and I was the pet, rather than the other way around. As long as I fed him and pet him when he was in the mood, all was good in our home.

"Morning, Newt," I said as I started my Keurig, then bent to get his bowl and food.

Once he was fed, I put my coffee in a to-go mug and headed out, locking up as I did. People here always said that they never locked their doors, it being a small town and me living out in a pretty remote area, but being from Philly, I was a compulsive locker.

As I was driving down Main Street, my eyes went to Three Sister's, as it always did, in hopes of catching a glimpse of Natasha. She was there, visible through their storefront window, sitting at a table by the window, alone, drinking coffee and looking down at something in front of her.

Rather than driving past and pulling behind Prime Beef to park as usual, I pulled in front of my restaurant, took a deep breath, and got out, and for the first time ever, I walked toward Three Sister's, intent on going inside and confronting Natasha once and for all.

I left my coffee cup in the car, figuring the pretense of getting coffee was a good enough excuse for going inside, although I'd never done it before.

If the girl behind the counter knew who I was, or if she was surprised that I was there, she didn't show it. Instead she welcomed me just as she did the other guests, and asked what I'd like to order.

Keeping my gaze forward, I had no idea if Natasha had noticed my entrance or not, since her back was to the door, and I found I needed a few seconds to try and calm my stormy pulse, before turning to her and approaching.

After what felt like mere seconds, my steaming coffee was in hand and I had no more reasons to stall, so I turned and started toward Natasha's table, then froze when I saw a man sitting across from her, smiling and laughing at something she said.

Raging jealousy filled me, and I was torn between storming over there and challenging the stranger to a fight, and fleeing before she noticed I was there.

I was about to flee when the option was taken from me as I heard a female voice say, "Jericho?"

Five

Natasha ~ Present

I whipped my head around, no longer hearing what Kalvin, my client, was saying, as soon as I heard Jericho's name.

It can't be, I assured myself. Jericho hadn't stepped foot into Three Sister's *ever*, there's no way he'd be there now.

Except, he was.

I nearly choked when I saw his long frame turning away from me to focus on the woman who'd called him. It was him all right, tall, dark, sinfully good-looking, *him*.

He was already dressed for work, even though it was breakfast time and his restaurant didn't open for another few hours. I noticed his hair looked perfectly tousled, and he was carrying one of our to-go cups.

I leaned to the side to get a better look, catching myself right before I toppled out of my chair.

"Hello, Mrs. Milstead, how are you?" Jericho was saying to the older woman who'd called out to him.

There was nothing covert about the way I was watching him. I was openly staring, gawking if you will, but luckily, he hadn't noticed. I was too shocked to be aware of what I was doing, or to really hear what they were saying, until, like a foghorn, I heard, "Are you ready to stop playing coy and let me set you up with my Belinda? I just know you two sweethearts will get along smashingly."

I must have gasped out loud, because Jericho's head swung my way.

I turned back in my seat so fast I almost got whiplash, and could feel the surface of my skin turning red with embarrassment. I hoped he hadn't seen me staring, even though I knew without a doubt that he had.

"Are you okay?" Kalvin asked, eyeing me with a knowing grin.

Kalvin and his fiancé, Malia, had hired us to cater their engagement dinner, and since Malia was currently away on business, Kalvin had been working with me to give them the engagement party of her dreams.

"Uh, yeah, sorry, what were you saying?" I asked, but Jericho was responding, rather loudly, and I tuned in to what he was saying.

"You know what, Mrs. Milstead, *yes,* I would love to take your daughter out. Why don't you give me her number and I'll set something up?"

My heart crumbled and I felt pain and anger radiating through me.

Did I have any right to be jealous? *Obviously not . . .*

Did I expect Jericho to be celibate since I'd left him? *Ha, just the thought is laughable . . . Jericho is an extremely sexual man.*

Does that mean it hurt any less to hear him making plans to go on a date with someone else, in my own place of business, no less? Nope, it hurt like a bitch.

Because, even if he hadn't been celibate, *I had,* and even if I didn't have a claim on him anymore, or the right to be jealous, I still was. *Very much so.* And although it didn't make sense, and my actions would lead people to believe otherwise, I was still in love with Jericho, and had a feeling I always would be.

What we had was that all-consuming love. The kind where no one else ever measured up, and I knew I'd never be as happy with anyone, as I'd been with him. But, it was also the kind that took over your life, your heart, your mind, and didn't leave room for anything else.

The destructive kind.

Which was why I stayed firmly facing Kalvin, unwilling to turn again and see if Jericho was watching me for a reaction

When I head the door jingle, signaling it had opened, Kalvin said, "He's gone," and I remembered how to breathe again.

"I'm sorry, Kalvin, could you excuse me for a moment?" I asked.

"Take all the time you need," he replied gently, and I felt the prick at the back of my eyes and knew the dam was about to break.

I'd barely closed the office door behind me before I lost it. Silent sobs choked me as tears ran down my face.

"*So stupid, Tasha,*" I chastised myself. "*Just forget about him . . .*"

Even as I urged myself, I knew it was impossible, especially now with Millie and Jackson getting married, and Jericho and Jackson being friends.

I needed to get over this, get over him, once and for all.

He'd obviously moved on, and it was time for me to do so as well.

I took a few deep breaths, wiped my face, and freshened up my makeup. While I reapplied my lipstick, I promised myself that I was done being a coward. I'd go and see Jericho and clear the air between us once and for all.

Then, hopefully, I'd have the closure I needed to move on.

Decision made, I went back out to finish my meeting with Kalvin with the intention of having dinner at Prime Beef.

I'd never been there before, and I heard the steak sandwich with chimichurri was divine.

"I'm so sorry about that, Kalvin," I said as I took my seat across from him.

"No problem," Kalvin assured me. "Did I ever tell you how Malia and I met?"

I shook my head and forced a small smile.

"We were both on dates with other people," he began, and I pushed all thoughts of my own romantic woes to the side to focus on Kalvin and Malia's happily ever after.

Six

Jericho ~ Past

I hadn't meant to ask her out.

I had a strict *no dating* policy. I was there to learn, get my degree, and get out. My only goals: building the restaurant of my dreams, owning a place of my own, and connecting with people who I could truly count on.

I hooked up with girls, sure, I was a college junior after all, and I hung out with my buddies, went to parties . . . experienced college the way it should be experienced, but I never went too far. I was always in control and cognizant of my goals.

Then this tiny brunette, clutching her backpack like a lifeline, bumped into me and refused to meet my eyes.

I thought she was naïve, delicate, adorable, and utterly irresistible.

I didn't know why, but I wasn't ready to let her walk past me and ignore me for the rest of the semester, so I left all of my belongings in the seat at the end of the last row and walked towards her until she bumped into me, then I maneuvered it so that we were sitting next to each other.

I found the way she laid out her school supplies just so totally charming, and her scent threatened my senses, so I knew I had to do something un-Jericho like and ask her out. No way this girl would be up for a night of just fooling around, hell no, she'd run fast in the other direction at the mere thought.

No, if I wanted to get to know *this* girl, and I did, I had to make an exception to my rule. I figured grabbing a cup at Coffee Time would be harmless enough, but I couldn't have been more wrong.

One cup of coffee and a little conversation, and I was a goner.

Natasha was sweet, funny, intelligent, and just as goal-oriented as I was. We talked about our upbringings, which couldn't have been more different, our families, and our futures. After the third cup of coffee, we switched to water, then decided to stop at the fast food joint next door for dinner.

If I had my way, I would have taken her back to my apartment and kept her there for eternity. Alas, she said she had to go back to the dorms and study, but promised to meet me again soon.

Which was why I was standing outside of her dorm like an idiot, holding a cup of coffee and a muffin.

I heard her before I saw her, her laugh causing the hair on my arms to stand up and my heart to gallop in anticipation.

There was a brief second where I worried that I was nearing stalker territory, then Natasha's head lifted and her gaze met mine, and her smile lit up my world. I watched as she said something to the girl she was with, then broke off and walked toward me.

"Hey," she said, somewhat breathless.

"Morning," I managed roughly, my face splitting in an unavoidable grin. "Breakfast?" I asked, holding up the coffee and muffin.

"That's sweet, thanks," Natasha said shyly, accepting the gifts from my hands.

"Can I walk you to class?" I asked.

"Sure."

"Would you like to go to dinner tonight?" I asked, unable to play it cool and wait. I knew what I wanted, so I damn well was going to ask for it. I'd lived too much of my life settling for less. Not this time.

Her cheeks flushed with pleasure.

"Yes," she replied. "Where? When?"

"I can swing by and pick you up at six," I said, then asked, "Do you like Italian?"

Natasha smiled. "Love it."

"Great, so, Italian tonight, and maybe Mexican tomorrow?" I suggested.

Natasha laughed. It was a beautiful, welcoming sound that I wanted to hear time and time again.

"Tomorrow?" she asked.

"Yeah, then Chinese on Thursday, Thai on Friday, and pizza on Saturday. Sunday, we can grill burgers, or hot dogs, if you like . . ."

Natasha laughed again.

"You've got the whole week planned out," she said with a smile.

"You can plan next week," I offered.

"That sounds like a lot of money. Maybe we should cook a couple meals at home, or eat at the cafeteria," Natasha suggested, and my heart soared.

She hadn't laughed at me, or looked at me like I was a creepy stalker. Instead, she seemed to be on board. I wondered if she felt the pull that I did, if she wanted to be with me as much as I wanted to be with her.

"Whatever you choose," I replied honestly. I'd eat a year of cafeteria food if it meant eating my meals with her.

"Hmmm, I'll have to think about it, but for starters,

yeah . . . Italian tonight, and Mexican tomorrow."

I hadn't kissed her yesterday, the timing hadn't felt right, and I didn't want to pressure her, but right then, in that courtyard, it felt like I *had* to kiss her. So, I stopped walking, and she did too, and when she turned to me, I placed my hands on her face, cupped it softly, and ran my thumb over her cheek.

"You're so beautiful," I murmured, taking in her flushed cheeks and sparkling hazel eyes, then I lowered my face toward hers, keeping my eyes open so I could watch as her pupils dilated. Her gasp hit my lips as she parted hers, and I brushed against them softly, before tilting my head slightly and deepening the kiss.

We kissed until we were lightheaded and feeling just a bit reckless, then I pulled back with a smile and chuckled when I saw her arms outstretched as she held onto the coffee and muffin so they wouldn't get crushed between us.

"Ready?" I asked, biting back a groan when she licked her lips and nodded in response.

I knew that she would be the death of me, and that I was really, *really*, going to enjoy the ride.

Seven

Natasha ~ Present

"Whoa, where are you going in those sexy boots?"

I was closing my door and looked up to the left to see Dru's head peeking out of hers.

Dru, Millie, and I all lived in the apartments above Three Sisters, giving us each our own space, while allowing us to be close by while we were building our business. Pretty soon, Millie would be moving out and into the house Jackson lived in with his daughter Kayla. They'd talked about buying a new house, but since Kayla had grown up there and they both loved the neighborhood, they'd decided to stay.

I thought it was weird, since Jackson had bought the house with his ex-wife, but if Millie didn't mind, it was really none of my business.

It would be weird not having Millie right down the hall, but we'd still get to see her every day at work, so I was okay. Dru was having a bit of a harder time coming to terms with it. She and Millie were twins, after all, and they'd never really lived apart.

We'd talked about using her apartment as a storage unit, like we did with the fourth space on the second floor, but had decided to rent it out instead. We didn't really need the space, and it would generate a little extra income, so we figured once Millie moved out, we'd clean it up and advertise it for rent.

I looked down at my ankle boots, then back up at Dru.

"They're not so sexy . . . more practical than anything," I tried.

Dru stepped out into the hallway, crossed her arms, and looked at me suspiciously.

"Practical?" she asked, dryly with a shake of her head. "Not so much . . . What's going on? You don't get dressed up like that unless we have an event, or are going out for the night."

I just stared at her, not wanting to say where I was going and have her make a big deal out of it.

"Please, tell me that you're finally going on a date," Dru said, putting her palms together and closing her eyes in prayer.

See, *dramatic.* Dru always made a big deal out of *everything.*

"No, no date, I'm just going to dinner . . . by myself."

Her eyes narrowed.

"Dinner. *By yourself,*" she mimicked.

"Yup," I replied.

"You don't like to do anything by yourself. Not shopping, not to the movies, not even to take out the trash. What's really going on? Where are you going to *dinner?*" she asked with air quotes.

Ugh, why does she have to be so obnoxious?

"Prime Beef," I mumbled, then turned and tried to hurry down the stairs.

"What was that?" she asked, rushing to me and putting her hand on my arm to stop my retreat. "Prime Beef? Are you meeting Jericho? What's going on? Have you talked to him?"

I sighed and turned to look at her.

"No, we haven't talked yet, that's why I'm going over there, to clear the air once and for all. Like Millie said, he'll probably be involved in the wedding, and this avoidance act is getting old. It's time for us to talk it out and put the past behind us. We're both adults, we can do this," I said, hoping I sounded more confident than I felt. "It's time to move on."

Dru's face softened and she squeezed my arm.

"Do you want me to go with you?" she asked.

"Yes," I admitted with a sharp laugh, "but I need to go alone."

"Okay, but I'll be here when you get back, and you'd better come straight to my apartment, or I'm coming to you."

I smiled at my sister and said, "Thanks."

She squeezed my hand again, then watched me worriedly as I gave a little finger wave and started down the stairs.

Prime Beef was just across the street, but it felt like I was walking the green mile to get there.

God, why is this so hard? Why am I such a big chicken?

I let a couple enter ahead of me, then gave a small smile when the man held the door open so I could enter. I walked inside and inhaled, taking in the delicious scent of fresh-baked bread as I walked into the entryway.

As I looked around, my first thought was, *Wow, he totally did it.*

Prime Beef was beautiful, and it was so totally Jericho. When we were dating, he'd often talked about his dream to open a restaurant and what it would look like. Looking around, it was exactly how I had pictured it.

"May I help you?" Pulled from my thoughts, I glanced to the hostess at the stand and stepped forward.

"Yes, um, just for one. Do you have a bar or something I could sit at, so I don't take up a whole table?" I asked.

I wasn't sure if Jericho would even have time to talk now, it being the dinner hour and all, but at least I was making initial contact. My hope was that he'd notice me and come talk to me, then we could set up a time to meet and talk for real. Otherwise, I'd enjoy my meal, then ask the server to talk to him afterwards, and try to set it up then.

"Of course, the bar is self-seating, so you can walk on back and sit wherever you'd like."

"Thank you," I said, and started in the direction she'd indicated.

I was almost to the bar, intent on ordering a stiff drink, when his voice from behind me stopped me in my tracks.

"Natasha," Jericho called softly.

Ah, my name, *said in that voice,* brought back a flood of memories that threatened to bring me to my knees.

I needed a minute to collect myself before I could turn and see him up close, so I stood there, facing the bar, as I struggled to breathe.

Eight

Jericho ~ Present

T watched as she walked across the street, one foot stepping slowly in front of the other, as if she were marching to her death. Then, as she debated whether or not to actually step inside of Prime Beef, I held my breath and waited. I saw her step inside and look around, and wondered what she was thinking.

I'd shared everything with Natasha. Often bouncing ideas off of her and asking for her opinion. I craved her thoughts in that moment.

I waited until she started toward the bar to come up behind her, and this time it was me struggling to find the courage to act.

At the sound of her name on my lips, Natasha stopped, but didn't immediately turn around. No, her shoulders lifted as she took a deep breath, and I could only assume she was steadying herself before she turned to face me.

It was that breath that told me she still cared, and I didn't even try to fight the hope that filled me with that knowledge.

"Natasha," I said again, my voice so low that only she'd be able to hear.

Finally, she turned, her eyes wide as she looked up at me. After a few moments, her lips parted, but no sound came out.

Terrified that she'd leave, I took control and asked, "Join me?"

I held out my arm, praying that Natasha would take it. When she did, I led her to a secluded table that we kept open for ourselves, or last-minute special guests. It was hidden in a little alcove, which would give us the privacy I knew we needed.

I held her chair out, before moving to sit across from her.

"A drink?" I asked, when she continued to look at me without speaking.

"Yes," Natasha said roughly, then cleared her throat and added, "Dirty martini."

I nodded at my server, indicating that I wanted my usual, and to get Natasha her martini. When he turned and left us alone, I folded my hands on the table and waited.

"I saw you . . . today, at Three Sisters," Natasha began. My gaze dropped when she began fidgeting with the napkin in front of her, and I bit back a smile at the evidence of her nerves.

She was as bad at this as I was, maybe worse.

"Yes," I replied simply. Even though I'd been willing to make the first move this morning, we were on my turf now, and I wanted to hear what she'd come to say.

"Why were you there?" Natasha asked boldly, her tone getting stronger.

"I came to see you, to talk things out once and for all," I admitted.

"Then, why didn't you?"

"I didn't want to intrude on your moment," I said, fighting to keep my voice even, so as not to give away the fact that seeing her with another man had caused me pain, even after all of these years.

"My *moment*?" she asked, looking adorably confused.

"The guy . . . the morning-after breakfast . . ." I managed, even though each word felt like razor blades in my throat.

Natasha's expression cleared and she chuckled lightly, then shook her head.

"Kalvin is a client," she explained, and my vision cleared. "We're catering his engagement dinner . . . to a woman who is *not* me."

"Oh, I'm sorry, I just assumed," I said, feeling like a fool. A relieved, very happy, fool.

"Anyway," Natasha began, letting out a deep sigh, then smiling at my waiter as he served our drinks. "Thank you," she said, then took a sip of her martini. "Delicious," she assured him, then looked back to me.

I held my scotch a little tighter than necessary and asked the question that I'd been dying to learn the answer to for the last few years.

"Why did you leave?"

Natasha put her drink down in front of her and cleared her throat.

"Millie called . . . My mother took a turn for the worse. I had to get to her, to spend whatever time she had left . . ."

"I understand that, Natasha," I said dryly. "I understood that then, and I still do. What I don't understand, is why it had to be like that. No goodbye, no note, no phone call, just . . . gone."

I didn't tell her that I'd sat in Coffee Time until lunch, waiting for her to show up, then went to her apartment, sure that she was sick or injured, only to find that it had been cleared out. She'd simply disappeared.

"I knew if I told you, you'd have offered to come with me, or asked me to come back . . . I knew you wouldn't let me walk out of your life."

"No, you're right about that, because it made no sense. It makes no sense. What did one thing have to do with the other? Why was it me, or your family? Why not both?"

My voice had started to rise, so I took a long drink of scotch and forced myself to calm down.

"I told you about my parents," she began, her eyes on the table, rather than me. "How my mother loved my father more than life itself, and he'd just left her . . . left all of us, for another woman, never looking back."

I nodded. We'd told each other everything.

"She never moved on . . . never recovered. I knew I had to leave you then, in that way, because I didn't *want* to leave you. My mother was dying and my sisters needed me, and all I could think about was being away from you. How I'd miss you, all the things I wouldn't get to do with you."

Natasha stopped when she started to get choked up, took a calming breath, and continued, "It hurt so bad, it felt like I was the one on my death bed. I wanted to call you, to go back to you, and I *knew* that I would . . . that once she passed and I helped Millie and Dru with everything, I'd go back to you."

"Why didn't you?" I asked, my own voice catching with emotion.

"Before she died, with her last breath, my mother called out to my father. The man who'd left her to raise three daughters alone, the one who'd broken her heart without a backwards glance, and she still yearned for him. I loved you that way, and that gave you all the power. The power to smash me into a million little pieces. So, I stayed. I finished my degree here and decided to go into business with my sisters."

"And smashed me into a million pieces," I said softly, not caring how those words made me look.

They were the truth.

"I'm sorry, Jericho, for all of it . . . Truly, I am."

I nodded.

"And now?" I asked, feeling worse than I had in years.

"Now, my sister is engaged to your friend, and there's going to be a wedding. Plus, we're business owners on the same street, in the same town. Is there any way that we could learn to be civil, to coexist?"

It wasn't what I wanted, but it was better than the avoidance of the past year. It was a start.

"Yes, of course," I answered, managing to sound unaffected, even though my soul was crushed.

Natasha gave me a small smile.

"Thank you."

I nodded, and she stood, so I stood with her.

"I'd better get going," Natasha said.

"I have to get to work," I agreed.

She smiled again and dipped her chin, then turned and walked out of the alcove.

I resisted the urge to pick up her martini glass and smash it against the wall. Instead, I downed my scotch and gave her a few moments to get out of the restaurant, then I went to check on my guests.

Nine

Natasha ~ Present

*T*he next couple of weeks flew by in a flash of fiftieth birthdays, wedding receptions, and Kalvin and Malia's engagement dinner.

We were so busy that it should have been impossible for me to let what Jericho said fester, but . . . fester it did.

And smashed me into a million pieces, he'd said, making me feel like the worst person in the world. I'd gone home that night, without dinner, and gone straight to Dru's as promised. Millie had been at Jackson's, so I cried on Dru's shoulder and we'd ordered a pizza.

I filled Millie in the next day, letting her know the talk had taken place, and we'd agreed to a truce. She'd been relieved, but I'd noticed her watching me warily ever since, as if she were waiting for me to break down at any moment.

I hadn't.

In fact, I'd even waved at Jericho when I saw him from across the street. Twice!

Still, that sentence had been on a loop in my brain ever since. Of course, I'd known I'd hurt him, but to think that by doing what

I thought was saving myself tremendous pain, only to cause *him* that pain, made me feel like a jerk of epic proportions.

"You ready?" Dru asked as she walked into our office.

Her eyes conveyed her concern, but she still managed to give me a reassuring smile.

"As I'll ever be," I replied as I rose from my desk.

This would be my first real test. We were meeting Millie and Jackson and Jackson's friends at the bar for a drink, kind of a pre-celebration celebration, for their engagement. The actual dinner would be held a week from tonight at Prime Beef, and would be a more formal affair, with tons of people in attendance. Tonight was just for friends and family. Which included me, and Jericho.

"I'll stay with you the whole time," Dru promised as we headed out.

"You don't have to do that," I assured her. "It's going to be fine. We talked . . ."

"Yeah, I remember," Dru said dryly, and I decided to let it go.

When we arrived at the bar, I was happy to see that we'd arrived before Jericho. Not that I was anticipating any problems, I just wanted to get settled and in my seat, maybe have a few sips of my drink before the comradery commenced.

"Hey, how's it going?" Rob, Jackson's friend and fellow teacher, said as we walked up. His wife, Jan, gave us a wave before going back to stealing fries off of Rob's plate.

"Ladies," Ty, another teacher and friend, greeted.

"Hi, everyone," Dru replied.

Jackson, Rob, and Ty all taught at the same school, along with Rebecca, Ty's girlfriend, who I saw standing at the bar. I waved at her, then took a seat across from Jan.

"The happy couple not here yet?" I asked.

"No, not yet," Ty said. "They were dropping Kayla off with Jackson's parents, and should be here soon. Rebecca's putting in an order of appetizers and getting a couple pitchers."

"What's up?"

I looked up to see a large man walk up to the table. I'd never seen him before. He was tall and built, like a UFC fighter or someone who did lots and lots of CrossFit. His hair was dark, and his face ruggedly handsome.

I turned my head and noticed Dru watching him, her eyes unblinking and her mouth hanging slightly open.

I kicked her under the table.

"Hey!" she cried, coming out of her trance and shifting toward me to punch me in the arm. "That hurt."

"Ow," I muttered, rubbing my arm and glaring at her. I lowered my voice and said, "I was trying to help you out before drool started dripping down your chin."

Dru flushed and said, "Shut up, I was not drooling."

"You sure as hell were staring at him like he's a medium-rare steak and you haven't eaten in weeks."

Dru rolled her eyes, then looked back at the man, before turning back to me and asking, "Did you see his eyes?"

I glanced at the stranger who was talking to Rob and Ty, his voice deep and rumbly. He must have noticed me staring, because his eyes flicked to me, and wowza, they were the palest green I'd ever seen. Truly striking.

Not knowing what to do, I lifted my hand and waved my fingers. "Hi, I'm Natasha, you can call me Tasha, and this is Dru. We're Millie's sisters."

"Hi," Dru squeaked, and I looked at her with surprise. She never got weirded out or intimidated by guys, ever.

The man rounded the table and strode toward us, his movements surprisingly graceful.

"Michael O'Donnelly, you can call me Mick," he said, his hand outstretched.

I took his hand first, since Dru was sitting there like a statue, and said, "Nice to meet you, Mick."

Once I heard his name, I remembered that he'd been the private investigator that Jackson hired to find his now ex-wife. Millie had mentioned that they'd become friends, and Mick had joined the fantasy football league and often met the guys for drinks.

"Nice to meet you, too," I said.

He released my hand and offered it to Dru, who stared at it like it was a stick of dynamite.

I kicked her again.

"Ouch . . . stop doing that," Dru complained, but it woke her up enough that she shook Mick's hand. "Hi."

They stayed like that for a minute, staring at each other in a way that had me feeling the need to fan myself, then Mick let her hand go and turned. I watched curiously as Dru's cheeks flushed, and was about to ask what the heck was going on when a movement caught my eye, and I looked up.

It was him.

Damn.

Apparently in the last couple weeks he'd lost his razor and missed an appointment with his barber, because his dark hair had grown out a bit and started curling around his neck, and he had the beginnings of the sexiest beard I'd ever seen.

Shit, I thought, as my heart started racing and my body warmed at the site of him. *He knows I love it when he starts looking a little shaggy, a little . . . dangerous.*

Was he doing it on purpose?

Ten

Jericho ~ Present

"How's it goin', man?" I asked Mick as I joined him at the bar. "Maker's neat," I told the bartender, then turned to the man who'd become a friend over the last few months.

"Another day, another case filled with bat-shit crazy people," Mick replied with a grin before taking a drink of his Guinness.

Mick was a PI and often dealt with the kind of people I'd grown up with, and, *yeah*, bat-shit crazy about covered it.

"Can you believe those two?" I asked, tilting my head toward Jackson and Millie, who were currently slow dancing in the middle of the bar. Led Zeppelin was on the jukebox and they were the only ones out there, but they were oblivious.

"Yeah, good for him after that waste of space he was married to before. It's a relief to see two decent people making it work, saves me from getting too cynical," he replied.

"Shit, you're the most cynical bastard I've ever met," I countered with a grin, but Mick just chuckled.

"Ain't that the truth."

I was about to follow Mick back to the group when I saw Natasha walking my way. I leaned back against the bar, trying to look casual as I watched her.

Beautiful as ever, her bright-red bob swayed around her face as she walked. Her makeup was smoky, and she was wearing a little black dress that showcased her body in an amazing way. A flood of memories assaulted me as she moved, eyes locked on mine, neither of us breaking contact.

"Hi," she said softly, her voice slightly rough, as if our little eye play had affected her as much as it affected me.

"Natasha," I said in greeting, dipping my chin slightly. "Can I get you a drink?"

"Oh, uh, we have pitchers at the table," she said, looking back over her shoulder.

I followed her gaze and saw that her sister, Dru, was watching us like a hawk.

"Beer?" I asked, memories swirling. "Did you develop a taste for it? I'm sure they have some Pinot Grigio behind the bar . . ."

Natasha flushed.

Yes, I remember everything, I thought.

"That sounds good," Natasha said, taking a deep breath before crossing to the bar and sitting on a stool. She surprised me when she nodded to the stool next to her.

Another olive branch . . . What would she think if she knew I wanted the whole damn tree?

I signaled to the bartender and took the offered seat.

"So," I began, turning my head slightly, so I could see her out of my periphery. "You know there's more to talk about . . ."

"I know," she said quickly, cutting me off, "but can tonight be about Millie and Jackson, about friends . . . about getting reacquainted? Please?"

Never having been able to deny Natasha anything, I replied, "Of course."

After a few beats, Natasha's wine arrived and she cupped the goblet and said, "Prime Beef is amazing, Jericho. Truly. It's exactly as I'd always pictured it."

I grinned, happy that she thought so.

"Thanks, Hector and I worked hard to make my vision a reality, and really, without his expertise in the kitchen, Prime Beef wouldn't be half of what it is."

"Hector? From when you were younger?" Natasha asked, and once again I was reminded of how much she knew about me.

"Yes. I got in touch with him before graduation and he had just started Le Cordon Bleu. Once I heard that, we started spit-balling ideas and came up with the plan to open Prime Beef together. We agreed on almost everything, the theme, the ambience, the food . . ."

"*Almost* everything?" she prodded. It was one of my favorite things about her, the way she paid attention, truly listening when I, or anyone, spoke. When she was with you, you knew you had one hundred percent of Natasha's focus.

It was a rare thing.

Although, in that moment, I found that I wished she hadn't caught that little detail. It was nice talking to her again, just hanging out, without the weight of the past. Without the questions. Without the reminder that she was no longer mine.

"Uh, yeah, the location . . . We disagreed about where to open it," I said softly, biting back a chuckle when she lifted her glass and took a big gulp. "Hector wanted to be in the city."

I saw by the look on her face that she regretted asking as well, regretted the fact that the easy, catching-up phase of this conversation was over.

"And you . . . ?" Natasha asked, although I could see the answer in her eyes.

"I came here for you," I admitted. When her eyes closed, I continued, "At least initially . . . you're what brought me here. But, when I saw the town, met the people, and looked at properties, I fell in love with the place. It's everything I never had growing up, and I completely fell in love with it."

Natasha nodded, understanding how I'd longed for something different than what I'd grown up with.

"And, Hector, is he okay with it now?" she asked, avoiding my confession.

"Yeah," I replied with a chuckle. "He loves it, actually. He's got his favorite fishing hole, loves the farmer's market, and has a great team in the kitchen."

Before Natasha could say anything else, Dru walked up behind us.

"Hey," she began, then caught herself and said almost kindly, "Hey, Jericho," before turning to her sister. "Millie wants us to play the Elvis Trivia Game with her."

Natasha groaned dramatically, causing me to chuckle.

"Seriously, again? Do we have to?" Natasha whined.

"It's her night," Dru offered.

"Hers and Jackson's, I'm sure he doesn't want to play Elvis Trivia."

"No, but he'd be all for Pride & Prejudice Trivia," Dru said with a laugh, and, yup, that was completely accurate. "But alas, the guys are playing pool."

"Jericho, you in?" Mick shouted from across the bar.

"Guess that's my cue," I said, hopping off the stool to get to the pool table before I got wrangled into Elvis trivia. "It was nice talking to you," I added sincerely.

"You, too," Natasha said with a small smile.

And as we walked in opposite directions, we kept our eyes on each other, just for a moment, and my hope of winning her back grew just a little brighter.

Eleven

Natasha ~ Past

*T*he first six months of school went by like a whirlwind, and it was all because of Jericho.

We'd spent every waking minute together. When I wasn't in class, I was with Jericho, and when I was in class, I was thinking about Jericho.

No, I didn't let my grades suffer; I still studied, I just did it *with* Jericho.

I didn't really get to know my roommates, because I was never in my dorm, choosing instead to spend my nights at Jericho's apartment. Not only was it nicer, had more room, and afforded us privacy, he had a kitchen.

We ate out often, but we'd recently found that we really enjoyed making meals together. I'd started checking out cookbooks from the library and we experimented with different dishes. It was fun, and added a whole new element to our relationship.

But tonight, I'd put together a meal all by myself. I wanted to surprise Jericho when he came home from class with a special dinner, and a special night.

It was our six-month anniversary. Six months since that fateful first day of class and our coffee date. I'd made steak, baked potatoes, and roasted asparagus, with a chocolate Bundt cake for dessert.

It wasn't only special because we'd been together for six months, but tonight I was going to tell him that I loved him, and I was also going to give myself to him. Like, *go all the way* . . . for the first time.

I was a little nervous, but mostly excited.

We'd obviously kissed a lot, and made out, and had done other things . . . things that made my body hot and tingly, and I knew it was going to be an amazing experience, I just had to convince Jericho of the same thing.

I knew he liked me, and I could obviously tell when he was turned on when we made out, but he'd never tried to push me into anything. I think he was worried that I wasn't ready. I mean, I knew that he wasn't a virgin. He'd been completely honest about his past, so I couldn't help worrying just a little bit, that it was my inexperience that kept him from taking my virginity.

Is it a turn off for him? Does he wish I were more experienced?

I didn't know, and couldn't bring myself to ask, so, tonight, I was taking things into my own hands.

I finished setting the table with my dollar store finds: a white tablecloth, two candlesticks with holders, and a pretty blue set of napkins, just as I heard Jericho's key in the door. My stomach gave a *whoosh*, as I waited for him to come find me.

"Tasha?" he called from the living room.

"Here," I replied, knowing all he had to do was peer around the corner and he'd see me.

I tried to lean casually against the chair, then felt foolish and stood up and clasped my hands together.

"Hey," Jericho began, then stopped and took in the room, and me.

I was wearing a slip of a dress, which was very short, and just a touch see through. I'd bought it specifically for this night, and hoped I looked as sexy as I felt. My body was positively humming with anticipation already, and he'd done little more than look at me in shock.

"What's all this?" he asked, his voice a touch rough.

"Happy anniversary," I said sunnily, then found my feet and crossed to give him a kiss.

I put my arms around his neck and looked up at him, sure that my love for him was written all over my face.

"I made a special dinner to celebrate," I told him, then tiptoed up to brush my lips across his.

Before I could pull back, Jericho took over the kiss, deepening it until my head got light. His arms snaked around my back, his hands coming to rest on my satin-clad bottom as he squeezed and pulled me closer. Close enough to feel his erection straining against his shorts.

I sighed and wriggled, trying to get closer, eager to feel his body against mine.

When he moaned, my knees started to buckle, my need for him swelling and expanding within me.

"Are you sure?" Jericho asked, moving his lips from mine to leave a trail of kisses down the length of my neck.

"Yes," I gasped. "So sure."

"What about your dinner?" he asked, and a thrill shot through me.

He doesn't want to wait until after dinner, that's a good sign, right? He's saying yes, and he wants me now . . .

I wanted to wrap my legs around him and secure me to him before he could change his mind. Instead, I tilted my head to give him better access and managed to say, "It's in the oven keeping warm, it'll hold."

I squealed as Jericho bent and put his hands behind my knees, swinging me up and into his arms. Then, his mouth was on mine once more as he moved us through the apartment and into the bedroom that we'd been sharing, chastely, over the past few months.

Jericho laid me down on the bed and got in beside me. He moved his kisses from my neck, across my shoulder, and down over my chest, before kissing my breast through the satin of my shift.

I arched my back and moaned; we'd gotten this far before, and it was one of my favorite things, having his hot mouth on my breasts, and when he sucked my nipples and bit down gently, I put my hands in his hair and cradled him close.

"Jericho," I said, urging him up. When he complied and was laying over me, his gorgeous face in mine, his hard body covering my length, I looked into his eyes and smiled. "I love you."

Jericho's eyes shut for a moment, as if he needed to freeze time and commit it to memory, then he opened them and grinned beautifully.

"I love you, too, Natasha . . . so much."

Twelve

Jericho ~ Present

"So, what's with you and Red?" Mick asked as we watched Jackson take his shot.

"They have a history," Ty answered, before I could say anything.

"Really?" Mick asked. "Lovers?"

I almost spit out my whiskey at that.

"Who the hell says *lovers*?" I asked with a chuckle, lowering my voice to mimic Mick's tone.

"Adults," Mick replied with a wink. "Did you want me to call her your *girlfriend*? 'Cause that's a lady right there."

"Well, when I met her, *girl* would have been a more apt description, but, *yes*, to answer your question, she's my love."

"Present tense," Mick noted, never one to miss a clue.

"At least they're on talkin' terms now, the last time we were here, it didn't go down as good," Ty added, then clapped me on the back and said, "Progress."

I nodded at Ty, then looked at Mick and said, "Yeah, present tense. At least on my end."

"Little Red's not feeling tall, successful, and brooding? Maybe she'll go for a yoked, rough and tumble, Irish Mick," he suggested with a chuckle at his own joke.

"Don't go there," I warned, the thought of Natasha with Mick causing red to flash before my eyes. Hell, not just the thought of her with Mick, the thought of her with anyone but me.

"Easy, Philly, no need to get out the boxing gloves, I'm just fucking with you," Mick said, taking a drink of Guinness and not looking the least bit worried by my warning. "I gotta say, if I was gonna dip my toe in *this* pool, Millie's twin seems like a firecracker."

"Yeah?" I asked, looking over my shoulder to where the women were sitting around a table playing trivia. Natasha and Dru were laughing at something Millie was saying, while the other ladies watched the sister with amused looks on their faces.

I could see the appeal, all three sisters were beautiful in their own right, and although Dru had never been my biggest fan, I always thought we'd get along great, based on the things Natasha had said about her.

"Why not go for it then?" I asked him, turning my attention back and noticing Jackson trying to get my attention. "Sorry, Jax, what?"

"It's your shot," he said patiently, a knowing smile on his face.

"What?" I asked as I walked to the table to take my shot.

"Nothing," Jackson said. "Just looking forward to watching this all play out."

I ignored him, focusing on my shot instead, then rounding the table to find my next one when I sunk the ball in the corner pocket.

"My frustration is entertainment for you?" I asked wryly as I passed him.

Jackson's grin fell.

"When we met, we were both a bit jaded and messed up from

the women who'd left us behind. Now, my ex ended up doing me a favor by leaving, and allowing me to find Millie, but you, Jericho, have a second shot with the one that got away."

I leaned on my pool stick and looked at my friend.

"Let's not get ahead of ourselves. Natasha only just started talking to me again a few days ago, and although my end game is to have her back in my life where she belongs, I don't think it'll be that easy."

"Well, I know you both individually, and I've seen the way you look at each other when the other isn't looking, so I'm going to go on record now and say that a happily ever after is in your future."

I couldn't help but chuckle at that.

As an English teacher, and a lover of classic romance novels, Jackson had always been a believer in true love, even when his ex-wife had left him and his daughter behind in order to go find herself, and he'd been heartbroken.

"You're such a romantic fool," I chided.

Actually, Jackson was one of my favorite people in the world, and one of the best things about him is that he's not afraid to be himself. He's one of the corniest people I know, and he's totally okay with it.

"Guilty as charged," Jackson replied with a smile.

"Get out of my way so I can take my shot," I said, shaking my head fondly at him.

When I missed my second shot and Ty was up, I went back to where Mick was half standing, half sitting on a bar stool, and resumed our conversation.

"So, as I was saying . . . why not go for it? With Dru."

"I don't mix business with pleasure," Mick replied vaguely.

"What do you mean, what business?" I asked, confused.

"I may run my own company, but I have a strict policy against sleeping with my clients. It has served me well thus far," Mick answered.

I turned to look at him and agreed, "That *is* a good policy, but I don't see what that has to do with Dru. She's not your client."

Mick shot me a bland look, but didn't say anything,

"Wait, she *is* your client?" I asked, looking back at the women again, as if they would give me the answer, then swung my head back to Mick.

"You know I don't discuss my clients," Mick replied, then went to go take his turn at the table.

I watched him for a moment, then looked over my shoulder and saw Natasha watching me. I smiled, but she just blushed and looked away, and I couldn't help but wonder why Dru would be hiring Mick, and if Natasha knew anything about it.

Thirteen

Natasha ~ Present

"I'm so glad we could fit this in today," I told Dru as we tried on our dresses for the wedding.

Millie and Jackson had decided against the traditional Maid of Honor and Best Man, and instead both Dru and I were standing with Millie, while Ty and Rob were standing with Jackson. Neither had wanted to have to choose between the four of us, instead wanting us to all be of equal importance.

Millie would be walking down the aisle with Kayla, since our father was as good as dead in our eyes, and our beloved mother couldn't be there.

"Ohhh, I like this one," Dru said. When I heard her dressing room door open, I opened mine to see which dress she'd tried on.

"That is lovely!" I exclaimed, stepping out and motioning for her to turn so I could see it all.

It was a fifties-style dress, falling just past the knees with a high collar and a flattering cut, in a pretty mint green.

"This color reminds me of Mick's eyes," Dru said, her tone just dreamy enough to have me snapping my gaze up.

"Oh, yeah?" I asked softly.

Dru's eyes widened, like she hadn't meant to say that out loud, then she cleared her face and shrugged.

"Yeah, sure, don't tell me you haven't noticed them, they're pretty unusual." She tried sounding nonchalant, but I wasn't fooled.

Before I could call her on it, she added, "It sure was nice of Jericho and Hector to offer to hold the engagement dinner, and allow us time to look for dresses today. Everything's going to go so fast with the wedding, since Millie and Jackson don't want to wait and want to get married as soon as possible, it's nice to be able to give up a little control, don't you think."

I narrowed my eyes at her change of subject.

"Mmmm, hmmm, it sure was," I replied dryly.

"I don't like that one," Dru said, pointing to the floor-length olive dress I had on.

"Me neither, toss that one over to me so I can try it on. If it looks half as good on me as it does on you, I think we'll have a winner."

"I wonder how Millie's doing?" Dru asked once we were both in our own dressing room.

Millie was in another section of the dress shop, trying on wedding dresses. We'd all broken off to find dresses that we loved, promising that once we had two or three that we loved, we'd meet in the middle to show them off.

Millie hadn't wanted to do the parade of dresses that some brides do when they are searching for the perfect dress, choosing instead to only show us her favorites.

"Here you go," Dru said, and I reached out to take the dress from her.

"I wonder how things are going at Prime Beef," I commented. Now that she'd brought it up, I couldn't stop thinking about it.

Usually, we were involved in every aspect of an event, and not being a part of setting up one of the biggest dinners in Millie's life was a bit stressful for me. I was kind of a control freak, and although I knew Jericho would do a wonderful job, it was hard not to be there.

"I'm sure it's great. Hector has a great menu planned, and Jericho has a full staff working nonstop to get ready. He closed the restaurant for the day to prepare, since just about the entire town will be in attendance, and although I may not be a hundred percent Team Jericho, I know he wants this night to be special for Jax and Millie."

"You're right, I know you are, I just get anxious," I replied, zipping up the back of the dress and turning to look in the mirror. I turned to one side, then the other, before turning fully and checking out the back side. "I think this is the one."

"Great," Dru replied, "I have on our number two. Let's go out and grab a glass of champagne while we wait for Millie."

We exited the dressing room and headed for the viewing area, where there was champagne, dark chocolate, and wafer cookies waiting. We poured ourselves a glass of champagne and walked to the set of large, floor-to-ceiling mirrors to check out our dresses once more.

Dru was wearing a high-low burgundy dress, which had a plunging neckline and was quite flattering. We twisted and turned, sipping carefully as we discussed the dressed.

"Don't the two of you look lovely," Margo, the owner of the bridal shop, said as she entered the area. "Are you ready to see Millie's choices?"

"Yes," I said excitedly, mentally clapping my hands together, since I couldn't actually do so with the champagne glass in my hand.

"So ready," Dru agreed, looking anxiously toward the bridal dressing area for her twin.

My breath caught when Millie walked in, her face flush with excitement. I could tell by the look in her eyes that she was in love, that this was the one . . . the dress she was going to be married in.

The sleeves and neckline were lace, delicately beaded, with an empire waist and a gorgeous cut that fit Millie beautifully.

"Oh my gosh, Mills," Dru gasped.

"You're the most beautiful person I've ever seen," I added.

"You like it?" she asked hopefully.

"Love it," Dru and I said in unison.

"Yay!" Millie exclaimed happily. "I love it, too."

She walked to the mirrors and sighed.

"It's just like what Priscilla wore when she married Elvis, except a bit more form fitting and modern."

Dru and I started laughing at that, because only our sister would choose the most important dress of her life by basing it off of Elvis's bride.

"Oh, I love the mint," Millie cooed when she caught my reflection in the mirror.

"That's our favorite, too," Dru informed her.

"Looks like we've made our decisions, Margo," Millie told the owner happily, then turned to face us and said, "Now someone get me a glass of champagne, please, this calls for a celebration!"

Fourteen

Jericho ~ Present

"I can't thank you enough, man," Jackson said happily. "Tonight is perfect."

Hector, our team, and I had worked all day to make sure everything would go seamlessly for Jackson and Millie's engagement dinner. Not only was it nerve-racking because he was a good friend and I didn't want to disappoint, but Millie and her sisters did this kind of thing for a living, and I wanted to help take some of the pressure off. Also, I'd be lying if I didn't add that I wanted to impress Natasha.

Hector had been a little concerned about closing down and losing two meals' worth of profits, but he was nothing if not a committed and loyal friend, and knew how much it meant to me to do this for Jackson.

Plus, things with Prime Rib were going so well, that the loss wouldn't do too much damage to our bottom line, and if it did, I'd cover it.

"I'm so happy you're enjoying yourself," I replied, clapping him on the back as we looked out over the dining room.

The party was in full swing. Dinner had been served and the guests were enjoying their after-dinner drinks in preparation for dessert.

"It's so nice having the space to have everyone together to help us celebrate. I can't tell you how much it means to me, *to us*, that you'd do this, Jericho."

"My pleasure, truly," I replied. "Anything to contribute to your happy day."

"Uh oh, I'd better go save Millie from Principle Wiggins," Jackson said, grinning at me over his shoulder as he walked off to save his fiancée.

"Jericho?" a female voice asked from behind me. I turned my head to see a tall, red-haired woman in a stylish suit standing behind me, her finger tapping nervously on her wine glass. "Jericho Smythe?"

"Yes," I replied, turning and offering my hand. "And, you are?"

The pretty lady took my hand and said, "I'm Belinda, Amelia Milstead's daughter. My mother said that she spoke with you the other day . . ."

It took me a minute, but then I remembered the morning in Three Sisters when I'd thought Natasha was on a date and had agreed to call Mrs. Milstead's daughter and ask her out. I'd completely forgotten all about it.

"Oh, Belinda, of course, how nice to meet you," I managed, wondering how I was going to get out of this without any hurt feelings. It wasn't that she wasn't lovely, she was, she just wasn't Natasha. "Are you having a good evening?"

"Yes," she said with a nervous laugh. "It's a great party. I'll have to keep Prime Beef in mind for my next event."

"Well, dinner parties we can manage," I said with a gentle smile, "but shutting down the restaurant is a once-in-a-lifetime event. My chef would throttle me if I tried to make it a regular occurrence."

Belinda made a humming noise in the back of her throat, then cleared it and began, "So, my mother . . ."

Knowing I needed to clear up the confusion I'd caused, I stopped her.

"Look, Belinda, I'm sure you're a great person, and lord knows, you're a beautiful woman, but . . ."

"But?" she asked, her expression conveying her disappointment.

"I'm afraid I'm not dating at the moment, and have no plans to in the future. I'm sorry that I told your mother that I'd call and ask you out, she kind of took me by surprise while I was in the middle of something, and I answered without thinking."

Belinda sighed.

"That sounds like my mom. I'm sorry if she's been bothering you, she's been on a mission for grandchildren for the last few years, and I'm afraid no eligible bachelors are safe. I appreciate you letting me know," she said, and began to turn away.

"Hey," I said, and she paused. "Don't worry about your mom; she's a great lady, no harm done. And, if you're ever in need of a friend . . ."

"Thanks," she replied, then walked away.

I turned back, thinking I'd better go check on Hector and make sure he wasn't planning my demise, and almost bumped into Natasha.

"Hey," I greeted, smiling in spite of myself.

She looked gorgeous, with her hair done in spunky curls, and her makeup smoky. I would have liked nothing more than to kiss the red off of her lips and divulge her of the sexy red dress she was wearing, but didn't think she was quite ready for that yet.

"You should take her out," Natasha said, and I didn't immediately understand what she was saying. Then she clarified, *"Belinda.* You should go out with her."

"I don't want to go out with Belinda," I replied, suddenly feeling a lot less happy.

"Well, you should. We've cleared the air and can finally put the past behind us and move on . . . Not that I'm saying you haven't moved on, I'm sure you have, multiple times, but I'm saying that you don't have to worry about my reaction. Or not date for my sake. We're both living here, and that's not going to change, you should get on with your life and take her, or someone else, out."

With each word out of her mouth, I grew more and more pissed off.

"You know, Tasha, I don't need you telling me who I should or shouldn't date. If I wanted to take Belinda out, I would, I don't need your permission. I also don't need you telling me how, when, or how many times I've moved on. You don't know anything about the last few years of my life, or where I am in it now, so I'd appreciate it if you kept your opinions to yourself."

With that, I moved around her and walked away, trying to keep an easygoing smile on my face as I moved through the dining room, when inside I was seething.

Before I went in the back, I swung around to see if Natasha was still standing where I'd left her, a few seconds giving me enough clarity to worry that I'd overreacted, but she was already gone.

Fifteen

Natasha ~ Present

I closed the door to my apartment and leaned against it, my breath coming in pants after running across the street and up the stairs.

He'd gotten so angry.

I sighed and fought back tears as I thought of Jericho's reaction. When I'd seen Belinda talking to him, I'd been hit with the pain of jealousy. Knowing that I needed him to move on, so that maybe I could, I thought I'd give him a little push . . . let him know that I would understand, but he didn't take it the way I'd thought at all.

I'd seen the pain my words caused, then the quick switch to anger.

I looked around my apartment. Sparse and humble as it was, it was no homier than my dorm room had been. No more lived in. While Millie and Dru had decorated their spaces with things they love, I'd never found the time to make this place anything other than a place to sleep at night.

It was depressing really, and being suddenly hit by a wave of loneliness only made it worse.

Maybe it's time for me to spruce the place up, make it look actually lived in. Get a pet or something.

Someone pounded on the door behind me, causing me to jump and squeal in surprise. I turned to look at the still-closed door, and knew who I'd find on the other side.

Shit.

I wiped my cheeks, put on a brave face, and opened the door.

"Hey," I managed, even though Jericho stood before me, seething.

I took a step back, then another as he started toward me, slamming the door behind him as he let himself inside.

I tried to back farther away, but he was there, taking me in his arms and lowering his face to mine. I opened my mouth to protest, and that was all the invitation Jericho needed.

It was like coming home, his lips on mine, familiar and oh, so wonderful. I sighed and practically melted against him as he deepened the kiss. My arms went up and around his neck, to steady myself, and to finally feel him. His hair in my fingers, his chest against mine, and his soft, supple lips.

Everything . . . this was everything. *He* was everything.

Sweet and sensual quickly turned to unbridled passion as the years apart disappeared and there was only now.

His hands were working on my dress as mine were unbuttoning his shirt, both of us eager to be skin on skin. Everything was on fire, and I worried if I didn't feel him, touch him, have him right then, I'd burn out.

"*Hurry,*" I said, desperate for him.

"You're driving me crazy," Jericho muttered, and then, we were free.

My hands eagerly roamed from his stomach, to his chest, then over his shoulders and down his arms. He was a little bigger, more muscular, than when we were younger, but was still, oh so familiar.

Years of not being touched in this way by another person had me writhing against him; the need to come was great, but the need to be with Jericho again, to be filled by him, was a visceral one.

He laid me back on my plain, brown sofa and covered my body with his. I opened for him, throwing one leg over the back of the couch, and the other I wrapped around his waist. We were consumed, obsessed, mindless to anything but the search for pleasure. For the connection that was always so damn good between us.

I was kissing his jaw, licking his earlobe, sucking on his throat, touching and tasting everything I could reach. It was like a madness had taken over and I'd given myself over to it.

I felt Jericho's knuckles brush against the front of my panties and I arched toward him, a whimper escaping my lips at the glory of that feeling. He moved his fingers down to push the delicate fabric to the side, then he was there. The tip of his cock teased my entrance and I moved my hands around to cup his still jean-clad ass and urge him forward.

"Please," I begged, too caught up in the moment to care how needy I sounded.

Jericho concurred, pushing inside until he was fully seated, then pausing with his eyes closed to enjoy the moment.

"Natasha," he breathed, and I knew he could feel how tight I was, how it took me a moment to become acquainted to his cock inside of me after all these years.

It felt amazing. *He* felt amazing. And I really, *really*, needed him to move.

I bucked up against him, which broke him out of his reverie and spurred him into action. I held on tight as he pulled out and thrust back in, over and over, faster and faster, until I was coming undone beneath him.

He wasn't far behind, coming with my name on his lips and rocking against me until we were both panting and exhausted.

All too soon, reality crept in, and what we'd just done hit me like a ton of bricks. Without realizing it, my body stiffened in Jericho's arms as panic threatened to suffocate me. I pushed him up and slid out from under him, falling to the floor in a tangle of graceless limbs, then shot up and ran to the bathroom.

"*Shit*," I whispered as I took in my flushed skin and messed-up hair. I was still in my bra and underwear. We hadn't even gotten naked in our rush to fuck.

I winced even as I thought it, because deep down, I knew that word could never be used to describe what Jericho and I did. We'd always been passionate. Since that first night together, we'd ignited something between us that I'd never imagined was possible.

I didn't know if it was a common occurrence, since I'd never been with anyone else, and I wondered if Jericho could tell.

Oh, how embarrassing it would be if he could. If he knew that I'd been pining over him all of these years, still in love with the man I'd left without a word. I knew I needed to come clean, really explain everything, not just gloss things over like I had at Prime Beef.

I'd been truthful about why I'd left, but not about everything since . . . not about how much I still love him, even though the thought of admitting it and being with him again terrified me.

Still, it was obvious that we couldn't go on the way we had been, so we needed to talk.

Really talk.

Resolved, I took a deep breath and opened the door, ready to lay my heart out and see what happened.

But when I walked out into the living room and looked around, I realized it was too late.

He was gone.

Sixteen

Jericho ~ Past

Natasha had given herself to me, and although I knew I was unworthy, I'd never cherished anything more.

We were lying in bed, and although we'd spent many nights in my bed before, everything had changed. She was mine now, and I was hers, and I vowed to myself that the ugliness of my past would never touch her. We would not repeat history. Instead, I'd give her a great life, an amazing life, and she'd never doubt how important she was to me.

"What does our future look like?" I asked, content to hold her in my arms as I played with a long, loose curl.

"Mmmmm," Natasha murmured, shifting against me.

I wanted her again. Just that one, small movement had me hardening, but it was too soon, so I moved slightly, not wanting her to notice my erection and think that meant I wanted anything more from her now.

I did, *God knows I do*, but I knew she must be tender, and was content to live in this afterglow for as long as she needed.

"A pretty house," she began, her voice low and sexy as all hell.

"Nothing too big or fancy, maybe a ranch style. I'd like a bit of land, so we can go for long walks at night, and plenty of space for our family to grow."

"Family?" I asked, liking the sound of that, especially in a place like Natasha described. As far away from the streets of Philly as you could get.

"Yes, of course, but that will come later," she said, and I could feel the curve of her lips against my chest. "First, we'll have pets."

"A cat, named Isaac Newton," I suggested with a chuckle.

"And a dog."

"What's the dog's name?" I asked.

"I don't know, I haven't met her yet."

"You have to meet the dog before you can name it?"

"Of course," Natasha said seriously. "It would be horrible if I named her Muffin, and then met her and realized she was obviously a Fiona."

"O-kay . . . What about the interior?"

"Big windows, so we can look out over our land, and a nice, state-of-the-art kitchen, that we can cook in together."

"What else?" I asked, enjoying the dream.

"Well, I don't collect anything like Millie, or obsess over flowers and stuff like Dru, but I've always liked the look of country-style homes. You know, lots of rich woods, rustic decorations, that kind of thing."

"Yeah?"

"Yeah."

"I could live with that," I said, thinking it was lightyears away from my mother's style of junkyard chic. I chuckled dryly at the thought. My mother had never given a shit about decorating, cleaning, or hell, cooking a meal. All she'd ever worried about was her next fix.

"Hey."

I shook myself out of my thoughts and looked at Tasha, who was propped up on one elbow, looking at me with a worried expression.

"Where'd you go?" she asked. "Were you thinking about your mom?"

God, this girl. She gets me like no one ever has.

"Yeah, sorry, don't you worry, that part of my life will never touch you," I promised.

"You know, I'd go with you, if you wanted to go see her . . . your mom."

"You're amazing for even suggesting it," I said, pushing her hair back off of her face and cradling it in my hand. "But I have no desire to see that woman. She didn't care about me enough to be there for me when I was growing up, and the only reason she's tried contacting me is because she heard about the money my grandfather left me. I don't want her anywhere near me, and I seriously never want you to lay eyes on her. She's in my past . . . you're my present and my future."

Natasha nodded and, sensing that I needed to move on from talking about my mother, said, "Well, I can't wait for you to meet mine. No doubt she'll take you in as her own and love you just as much. And, Millie and Dru, you're going to love them."

"I'm sure I will. From as much as you've talked about them, I feel like I already know them."

It was true, her family sounded great. Well, except for her father, who seemed about as useless as my parents. Still, we'd been so happy in our little bubble together, it was hard to imagine what our lives would be like with other people involved.

"Do you want to live there, near your family?" I asked. So far,

Natasha had never mentioned wanting to go back, but the dream home she described sounded like it would fit in perfectly in her hometown.

"I don't know," she said with a shrug. "It doesn't really matter to me where we go, as long as you're there, but when you've talked about your restaurant, I've always gotten the feeling that you were picturing it in a big city."

"We could always live outside of the city on some land, and get the best of both worlds," I suggested. "I agree with what you said, though, as long as we're together, I don't care where we live. I can compromise, all I care about is your happiness."

I took her in for a moment, the tousled hair, full lips, and rosy glow, and had the sudden urge to see her fall apart for me once more.

Shifting, I moved her onto her back and covered her body with mine. Nuzzling her nose, I kissed her lips gently and said, "It's too soon to have you again the way I want, but that doesn't mean I can't make you come."

I felt the change in her breathing, saw the heaviness of her eyelids, then the sexy curve of her lips.

"What did you have in mind?" Natasha asked throatily, laying back against my bed and offering herself up to me.

I kissed my way over her breast and down her stomach.

"How about I show, not tell," I offered, nipping her belly lightly.

"Show me," she breathed, as I settled between her legs and complied.

Seventeen

Natasha ~ Present

"Just text me the directions," I said, then hung up on my soon-to-be brother-in-law, not ready to answer the twenty questions that came from me asking for Jericho Smythe's address.

As soon as I realized he was gone, I quickly got dressed and headed out to find him.

My first guess had been Prime Beef, but after I ran around back and saw that his car was gone, I figured it was best to drive out to his house and see if he was there, rather than go back into the party filled with everyone I knew in the world, and suffer through all of their questions.

I heard my phone ping and picked it up to look at the directions Jackson had sent. It was a small town, so I knew exactly where the street he'd sent me was located. I made a U-turn and pointed my car in that direction, nerves igniting in my stomach as I realized that I'd be there in less than ten minutes.

Once I found the house number on the mailbox, I turned left onto a dirt road and followed it back, gasping when I broke through the trees to see the house seated about a half mile off the road.

It was cute, quaint even, a one-story ranch-style home with a wraparound porch and a white picket fence surrounding it. The kind of fence that would hold a dog in the yard when necessary, or keep your children from running wild on the land. And, what beautiful land it was. There were large trees crawling across the acreage, as well as a few fruit trees, blooming with blossoms, and rose bushes on one side of the house.

It was like a dream come true. *Our* dream come true.

I parked next to Jericho, so I knew he was home, then got out, my head swinging back and forth to take it all in as I walked up to the front gate, opened it, and let myself inside. My breath caught as I walked up the steps of the porch to knock on the front door, and waited.

After a few short, agonizing moments, the door swung open to reveal a shocked Jericho standing before me. He'd already changed out of his work clothes and into some basketball shorts and a T-shirt that said, *come to the math side, we have pie*, except it was the pie symbol, not the word.

"Natasha," Jericho said, then gestured with his hand and added, "Please, come in."

I tried to give him an apologetic smile as I walked past him and into his house. Rather than pausing just inside the door, I took in my surroundings and walked farther into the house. When I stepped down into the living room, I gasped as I took in the open area, which looked up into the kitchen, both of which were decorated with rich woods, and had a down-home, country feel. I could see the gleaming, state-of-the-art appliances from where I stood, and turned to look at Jericho, my mouth open with shock.

"What did you do?" I whispered.

"Natasha, I'm so sorry," he began, taking a step toward me then stopping abruptly, as if he wanted to reach for me, but was afraid to. "I'm sorry for leaving like that, for not staying and facing you like a man, but I was so ashamed."

"Wait . . . what?" I asked, because while I was talking about the fact that he lived in the home we'd dreamt up together, he was obviously talking about something else. "Face me about what?"

"I saw the look on your face . . . after. And, *God*, Tash, if I took advantage, or forced you to do something you didn't want to do . . ."

Oh, no, no wonder he'd left.

"No, Jericho, I promise, that wasn't the problem at all. I was there with you, one hundred percent."

Jericho ran a hand over his hair, his eyes searching my face.

"You were?"

"Couldn't you tell?" I asked shyly, taking a step closer to him, until I was less than an inch away from touching him. I looked up and said, "I'm sorry I freaked. I was shocked at my behavior, then embarrassed that I'd attacked you like that, that it was obvious it had been a long time . . . and, finally, I was worried that we'd ruin the friendship that we'd just started to rebuild."

Jericho's hand came up slowly, tentatively, before he placed it against my cheek, his thumb caressing me sweetly.

"How long?" he asked gently.

Of course, that would be the part he'd focus on.

I took a deep breath, and knew I had to be honest. "Since the last time . . . with you."

Jericho closed his eyes, then opened them and smiled wider than I'd ever seen.

"For me, too," he said, and I was sure I heard him incorrectly.

"You can't mean . . ."

He nodded and lowered his face to mine, his lips barely brushing mine before he pulled back.

"There's been no one else," Jericho admitted. "I told you, you're it for me."

This time I closed my eyes and leaned forward. He kissed my forehead and waited for me to gather my thoughts.

Once I had, I leaned back and brought my hand up to grasp his wrist at my neck.

"This house?"

"I bought it for you . . . for us," he replied.

I didn't know what to do with all of the thoughts and emotions swirling within me. I was afraid to give myself over to him completely, but after what had happened at my place, and what we'd just admitted to each other, I didn't think I had a choice.

Plus, he'd made our dream house a reality, even when he had no idea whether we'd grow old in it together, or he'd live there all alone.

I owe it to both of us to give it a shot.

Before I could say that, I felt something brush against my leg and looked down to see a black cat walking between us.

I looked up at Jericho with a grin and asked, "Isaac Newton?"

Eighteen

Jericho ~ Present

J couldn't believe she was there, that she'd come after me. I tried to keep my cool, not make assumptions, because God knew I'd been burned by Natasha in the past, but it was useless. Having her here, in the home we'd imagined, in my arms, smiling up at me, filled me with all the hope in the world.

Call me foolish, but it couldn't be helped . . . I was a fool for Natasha. I always had been.

"Yup, that's Newt," I replied, my chest tight at the way she was looking at me. Her face filled with wonder.

"I can't believe you did all this," Natasha gushed, looking around my home once more. "I thought you'd move on, that you'd forget."

I shook my head, hoping she'd hear my words and take them to heart, once and for all.

"Natasha, you're it for me. I knew it when you walked into accounting class and bumped into me, I knew it when I realized you'd left, and I *know*, that's how it will *always* be. No matter what you do, where you go, or how you choose to live out the rest of your life, for *me*, there is no one else. I'm not looking for anyone else, and I don't *want* anyone else."

Her eyes were wide on me, so I asked, "Does that scare you?"

"Terrifies," she admitted, but she wasn't running. She was still in my arms, so, that was progress.

"I can wait until you get used to the idea," I promised. "If you think you're willing to give us another shot, whether tomorrow, or a year for now, I'll wait. I'll give you time. Space. Whatever you need. You've got it."

"Thank you," Natasha whispered, and I had to know.

"Does that mean you are willing to give us another shot?" I asked gently, trying to keep the excitement out of my voice.

Natasha nodded slowly, and I let out a sigh of relief.

"But . . ." she began.

I took her hand in mine and brought it to my lips, kissing her palm softly.

"What do you say I pour us a drink and we sit out on the back patio and talk. Tell me what you're worried about. Let's get it all out there and start fresh."

"That sounds perfect," she replied.

"Make yourself at home, look around, and I'll get those drinks."

I pulled a bottle of chilled Pinot Grigio out of the wine fridge. *Yes*, I kept it stocked, because I'd always held out hope that this day would come, then grabbed the bottle of Maker's Mark from the cupboard, and set about preparing our drinks.

"I still can't believe all this," Natasha said as she joined me in the kitchen.

"Do you like it?" I asked, practically holding my breath while I waited for her answer.

"It's perfect," she replied with a smile.

I knew it was too soon to let her know that if she wanted to make any changes to the house, the land, or . . . anything, all she had to do was say so, and it was done.

So, rather than freak her out I said, "We'll go out those doors there, there's patio furniture on the back porch."

She opened the sliding glass door and stepped out. As I walked out behind her, I heard her intake of breath, then she said, "This is amazing."

I looked at the comfortable patio furniture, with oversized cushions and plenty of sitting room, with a fire pit in the middle, and tables strewn around. In the daylight, there was a beautiful view of the pond and the trees, but for now, Tasha was just looking at the porch.

"Thanks," I said, pleased that she liked it, since everything in this house was bought with her in mind.

I sat on the loveseat, and Natasha sat in the chair next to it, which was turned a bit to the side so that we could be face to face while we talked. Once she was settled, I handed her the glass of wine, then settled back into my seat.

"*But*," I prompted, wanting to pick up where we'd left off.

"Like I said at Prime Beef," Natasha began. "After my mom passed, I was afraid that I was just like her, destined to love someone so much . . . to love *you* so much that if anything happened to you, or you left me, I'd never be able to recover. So, I did kind of a preemptive strike, and decided to leave you before things got even more serious between us."

"I think things were already as serious as they could be," I put in, my heart still raw at the memory.

Natasha looked at me sadly.

"Yeah, I guess that's what I found out. I was devastated, and I missed you terribly, and the thought of meeting someone else was never even an option. So, yeah, it was already too late. We'd already found each other and the damage had been done. *But*, I also found out that my life wasn't over because we weren't together. I still had my sisters and we opened this business together, became successful, and I was able to be happy."

Even as her words hurt, I wanted that for her. I wanted her happiness.

"But . . . it's only a modicum of happiness. There's something missing. And, although I now know that I can live a life without you, I also know that it's not a *full* life. I've missed you, and as much as I've tried to push you away and keep my feelings at bay, I know with you, I can be truly happy."

I waited, wanting to let her say everything she needed to before butting in with my own thoughts and feelings.

"After seeing Millie and Jackson, and talking with you a little bit, and what happened tonight, I can't fight it anymore. *Yes*, I'm still a little skittish, and I'm afraid of losing who I am now when we're together. Because when I'm with you, I tend to get overcome with you, and a little lost in you, and I don't want to get swallowed up in my feelings again."

Natasha took a sip of her wine, then, realizing I'd been uncharacteristically quiet, looked at me and reached a hand out for mine.

I took it, enjoying the feel of her soft skin beneath my thumb.

"I need to find balance," she admitted softly. "Do you think that's possible?"

Natasha ~ Present

I waited and watched Jericho's face, hoping his answer would be the one I wanted. The one I needed, because as much as I wanted to be with him, what I said was true, I needed to find the right balance between my worlds, and find a way to merge them all together without any part being left out.

Jericho leaned forward and took my hand in his, running his thumb over the top.

"Of course I think it's possible," he replied, and my stomach unknotted. "Natasha, I don't expect you to give up everything and live only to be with me. I'm not going to lock you up in this house and keep you for myself."

"I know that," I began, then stopped. He'd let me say what I needed to, so I'd do the same for him.

"Natasha, we're older now. Adults with our own businesses, our own friends . . . that doesn't need to change because we're together. Yes, when we were young and in school, it was easy to forget everything and everyone else and focus solely on each other, but now we have a different set of responsibilities. Will we get to see each other as much as we did back then, no, probably not, at least not at first, but that doesn't mean that when we are together that we can't give each other what we need."

I nodded, knowing he made sense, but still a little worried about how I'd handle adding Jericho Smythe into the mix.

"I'm not saying it won't be challenging, but, Natasha, we *can* make it work. I know we can. Yes, we're busy, and there's a lot going on right now, but we'll figure it out. We're smart, capable individuals. I have faith in us," he added with a really cute grin.

"Okay," I replied. "Let's do this."

Jericho sat back and picked up his drink, a content expression crossing his face. He turned his dark eyes to me and asked, "Stay with me tonight?"

"I didn't bring anything with me," I stated, even though the thought of staying the night had my body tingling.

"I have stuff you can use," he replied.

I nodded and sat back to enjoy the rest of my wine.

"So," he began as he settled in and looked at me fondly. "What do you think of Millie and Jackson getting hitched?"

I smiled, realizing how much I missed just *talking* with Jericho. He'd always been a great sounding board.

"I'm so happy for them. Before he came along she was happy. Happy in her kitchen and with our business, but since she met Jackson . . . Millie practically glows with happiness. Things were a little rough with Kayla at first, but now, she fills a hole Millie didn't even know she had. I love seeing the three of them together, and I think Jackson is *the best*."

"He is, and after what his ex put him through, he deserves someone like Millie. They really complement each other well, and I've never seen him so happy either. I don't know if I'd say he *glows . . . but . . ."*

We both laughed.

"They deserve each other," he stated, and I nodded in agreement.

"And what about Dru? Am I crazy, or is there something going on with her and Mick?"

That stumped me.

"Huh?" I asked, utterly baffled. "Dru and *Mick*? I don't think they've ever even said more than two words to each other. I mean, she obviously thinks he's hot, because he is." Jericho raised his eyebrow, but I just laughed. "But, as far as I know, they don't know each other."

"Hmmmm," was Jericho's reply.

Needing to know what he seemed to, I jumped up and joined him on the loveseat, turning toward him and punching him lightly on the arm.

"What do *you* know?" I asked.

He turned toward me, his eyes twinkling in the light, his face gorgeous with happiness.

"Well, when we were at the first engagement dinner the other night, I noticed them eyeballing each other and Mick may have suggested he was interested, but when I said he should go for it, he said something strange."

"What?"

"He said he had a strict rule against dating his clients, well, he may not have said, *dating*, but you get the idea."

"Clients?" I asked, confused. "You are talking about Mick O'Donnelly, the PI, right?"

"That's the one."

"But, why would Dru need a PI?"

Jericho lifted a shoulder and said, "I think your sister's the only one who could answer that."

"Huh," I muttered, but my mind was already running wild. There was only one reason I could think of that would cause Dru to hire a private investigator. I didn't like it one bit, and I know Millie wouldn't either. And, although I hoped I was wrong, deep down I knew I wasn't.

"You okay?" Jericho asked, his arm coming around my shoulder.

"Hmmm, oh, yeah, I'll be fine," I replied, chewing on my lower lip as I worried. "It's just, the only thing I can think of, is that she's trying to find our father."

Jericho pulled me in close, knowing how much I hated my father for what he did to my mother, and to us, and when we were together I'd told him repeatedly that I never wanted to see that man again as long as I lived, but apparently my sister didn't feel the same way.

Twenty

Jericho ~ Present

"Natasha has a meeting this morning, and two more this afternoon, but she's going to try and stop in for lunch. I was hoping you'd join us," I told Hector as I watched him prep for today's lunch meal.

"Why?" Hector asked, not looking up at me.

"Hector," I said, waiting for him to acknowledge me. When he didn't, I added, "Look, I know Natasha isn't your favorite person . . ."

"Understatement," he said dryly.

"But," I went on as if he hadn't spoken, "you know how important she is to me."

"I also know what she did to you," Hector said, still not looking at me, the ass.

"We're going to give this thing another try. Hector, you know how much I want this, that she's *the one*. Please."

Hector finally looked up, his expression pissed as he pointed his knife at me.

"I was there to pick up the pieces when she left. You were too fucked up to know what that looked like, but I remember with a hundred percent clarity. I get that you're excited and happy that she's back in your life, but I need a little more time."

"Seriously?" I asked, getting pissed even though I understood his reasoning. "So, you won't have lunch with us?"

He shook his head. "I don't think it would be a good idea. It wouldn't go the way you have planned in that big heart of yours."

I sighed. I realized it was ridiculous to get mad at the one person who'd been there with me through every shitty situation in my life, but I'd been so eager to get the two of them together . . . finally, that it hurt when Hector said no.

"Okay," I said, my anger leaving as swiftly as it entered. "I get it, but I'm not giving up. She's not going anywhere and neither are you, so you'll have to come to terms eventually."

"I hope so, for your sake," he replied, and I knew he was talking about her sticking around.

I pushed down the anger that was threatening to bubble back up, instead turning on my heel and heading for my office.

I couldn't fault Hector for having my back, it just sucked that my dream of my two favorite people loving each other as much as I loved them, would take a lot longer than I'd anticipated.

If it happened at all.

I'd barely crossed the threshold when my phone rang.

Seeing it was Natasha, I picked it up with a grin and said, "Hello, beautiful."

"Hey, Jericho," she replied, and I swear, I could hear the smile in her voice. "I have some bad news."

"What's that?"

"My second meeting got pushed up, so I won't be able to come by for lunch."

"No problem," I replied, disappointed, but as I looked at my list, I realized I could get a lot more done if I ate lunch at my desk. "Come by for dinner?"

"Actually, we're helping Millie pack tonight, and were planning to order pizza," Natasha replied. I could hear her voice getting tense, and knew she was starting to worry about that balance she wanted to find.

"How about this, you guys skip the pizza and I will have one of my guys run over dinner for you and your sisters. Once you're done, you can send me a text, and either I'll come to you, or you can come to me."

"That sounds amazing, much better than pizza. Thanks, Jericho."

"No problem, babe," I replied.

"See you later."

"Bye."

No sooner had I hung up, then my phone dinged, signaling a text.

O'Reilly's tonight?

It was from Jackson.

I'm in, I replied.

Great, you can tell me what happened the other night.

The other night?

Yeah, when I texted Natasha your address after you both disappeared during my engagement dinner.

Sorry about that . . . Are you going to be painting our nails and watching The Real Housewives as well?

Stop trying to change the subject. As her soon to be brother-in-law, I need to know your intentions. Come prepared to spill.

Just us?

Nah, all the guys will be there. We're talking Bachelor party tonight.

Perfect, see you later.

I chuckled, even though I knew Jackson could be relentless

when he wanted information. The realization that one day, we could actually be related by marriage, literally warmed my heart. He was a great dude, the best, and as a man who had no family, the thought of actually having some filled me with something that was hard to name.

I mean, yes, I had Hector. But having Natasha, and gaining her sisters, and Jackson and Kayla as well, was almost more than I'd ever hoped for.

So, as I worked my way down my list, checking things off and eating at my desk as I did, it was with a smile on my face and a burst of hope in my heart.

Twenty-One

Natasha ~ Present

"Wow," Dru said as she looked around Millie's now sparse living room. "I can't believe you're actually moving out."

We'd spent the last few hours packing up Millie's belongings, and were currently sitting on the floor, enjoying the generous spread Jericho had sent over from Prime Beef. There was a salad, a delicious roasted chicken, with asparagus and fingerling potatoes.

So much better than pizza, I thought with a smile.

"I know," Millie said with a sigh as she picked up her asparagus and took a bite. "Tomorrow the movers will come and it will be official." She looked around the room, then back at us and added, "You guys, I've never lived with a boy before. It's going to be so weird."

Dru chuckled and said, "Sexy weird. You're going to love it." Then she nodded her head toward me and asked, "What's this one so happy about?"

Millie looked at me knowingly and replied, "She went to Jericho's the other night, after the two of them disappeared from our party."

"Sorry about that," I said, feeling guilty for leaving her

engagement party like that.

"Oh, stop, we'd already had the party for family, and you didn't miss anything by ducking out early. What I want to know is, what happened between you and Jericho after you left?"

"You may as well just spill, Tash, you know how Millie gets when she wants information," Dru said, then looked down at her food and added, "Although I'm guessing what ever happened was pretty good, since we've never gotten delivery from Prime Beef before."

I took my time before answering, drawing the tension out a bit, since I never had any news to spill. It was always Millie and Dru with the good stuff.

"Well, I'd overheard him and Belinda at the party. Her mom had tried to set them up, but Jericho never called and he was letting Belinda down easy. Thinking I needed to give him the green light, I told him he should go for it, and he got really mad. I left in a bit of a snit and went back to my apartment, and a few seconds later he was pounding on the door. As soon as I opened it, he jumped me."

"Ohhh, angry makeup sex, years in the making . . . tell us everything," Dru said, leaning in as she popped chicken in her mouth as if it were popcorn.

I laughed, the memory making me blush as I thought of how desperate we'd been for each other.

"Anyway, yeah, it was hot. Sex between us had always been good, but that night, it was like . . . uber hot. But, as soon as we came down from the high, I was mortified. After a year of ignoring him and weeks of telling him we could only be friends, I'd hopped on him like a ride at Disney and threw caution to the wind."

"Nice," Millie whispered, fanning herself.

"I freaked and ran to the bathroom, needing a little space to get myself together, and when I came back out, he was gone."

"Jeez, you guys are like a soap opera," Dru said, laying down on her stomach and placing her chin in her hands. "What happens next?"

"Well, this time I followed him. I got his address from Jackson . . ."

"Which is how I knew," Millie put in.

"Then took off after him. And, when I got there, *you guys* . . . his house. It was everything we'd ever talked about when we were together. Our dream home. He found it and has been living there, waiting for me to get my head out."

"Really, that's so sweet," Millie gushed.

"Yeah, yeah, get back to the good stuff. What did he say when you showed up?" Dru asked.

I chuckled at my sister and said, "He was surprised, but let me in. He'd thought when I ran out that he'd been too aggressive, or had taken advantage of me. So, we talked it out."

"You two are like *Three's Company*. You need to talk your shit out," Dru said wryly.

"So, what did you decide?" Millie asked, ignoring her twin.

"We decided to give it a try. *Really*, give it a go. He knows I'm nervous about losing myself, about turning out like Mom and giving him everything I have, only to have him leave me. But, that fact is, he's never left me, I was the one who left. He said that he's known I was it for him since we met in college and that there hasn't been anyone else but me and never will be."

"You mean, all these years?" Millie asked, then sighed dreamily. "Oh my God, that's so sweet."

"I know, and although my brain hears everything he says, and I know the proof is right there in front of me, he's proven that his intentions are true. It's just, in my heart . . . in my gut, I'm terrified. I mean, already today we were supposed to have lunch and I couldn't, then he asked me to dinner, and I already had plans."

"Did he get mad?" Dru asked.

"No, not at all, in fact, it was his idea to send us dinner, and he wants us to spend the night together. It's not him, you guys, it's me. I feel myself getting consumed by him already. *I* hated that I had to skip lunch, and that I couldn't see him for dinner. I miss him, and I find myself wishing I didn't have these other meetings and appointments getting in my way of spending time with him. This is just what I was worried about, what if I can't find the balance in my life?"

"Oh, honey, that isn't you not finding balance or being consumed by someone else. There's nothing wrong with wanting to spend all of your time with Jericho. That's *love*. I felt the same way about Jackson. Don't you remember, you guys made fun of me for wanting to hire more people, so that I could free up time to be with him."

I did remember, although I'd never compared it to my feelings for Jericho. Maybe they were right, and I was overreacting.

"Yeah," Dru agreed. "You're not in danger of being like Mom, you're just a woman in love."

Twenty-Two

Jericho ~ Present

"Okay, while he's in the bathroom, we need to discuss the *real* bachelor party," Rob whispered, leaning in close and urging the rest of us to do the same.

We were at O'Reilly's and had just finished a round of beer and wings while discussing a weekend bachelor trip to Vegas. It seemed like an odd send off for Jackson, who seemingly had no interest in gambling, strippers, or the desert, but he was happily going along with everything Rob and Ty had thrown at him.

"What real bachelor party?" I asked.

"Well, it's not just going to be us, it's going to be a joint Bachelor and Bachelorette weekend, and we aren't going to Vegas . . ."

"Where are we going?" I asked, looking to Mick, who shrugged, as out of the loop as I was.

"First, we are going to tour the Emily Dickinson Museum, then road tripping about seven hours to Boonsboro, Maryland, where we'll stay in Nora Roberts' hotel, the Inn Boonsboro." Rob's voice began to rise, the more excited he became.

"Yeah, and while there, Jackson and Millie can stay in the

Elizabeth and Darcy room." Ty looked at Rob, who nodded back at him and added, "He'll be beside himself. We can either stay there in the themed rooms too, or go somewhere cheaper in town, depends on our budget . . . then, the next day there's a book signing at Nora's husband's bookstore. After which, we'll road trip back home."

"I'm out," Mick said, at the same time I asked, "Who's Nora Roberts?"

"You're out?" Rob asked, narrowing his eyes suspiciously. "It's the same weekend we were doing the Vegas trip, and you *just* said you could make it."

"I'm free for Vegas, but this book tour stuff . . . something just came up," Mick stated.

"Not even for Jackson?" Ty asked.

"Not even for the Virgin Mary," was Mick's reply.

"Jan and Rebecca can't go either," Rob said, then looked at me, "What about you, Jericho?"

"I'm in," I replied, thinking a road trip with friends, and Natasha, sounded fun. To Vegas or the moon, I didn't care. "And, don't worry about a budget, I'll cover it. It'll be my wedding present to the happy couple."

"You'll cover what?" Ty asked.

"The trip."

"For Jackson and Millie?"

"For everyone."

"*Everyone?*"

I chuckled and took a swig of my beer.

"Yeah, don't sweat it, send me the details and I'll handle it."

Ty's eyes swung to Mick.

"Still not in," Mick said.

"Not in what?" Jackson asked as he came back to the table, a bucket of beers in his hands. "I stopped at the bar for another round. What are we talking about?"

"We were giving two to one odds that Ty would propose to Becca by April, but Mick said he's not in . . ." Rob lied.

"What?" Ty screeched.

"Yeah, it's a fool's bet," Mick added with a grin. "He's definitely the type to propose at Christmas."

"*What?*" Ty repeated.

"I'll take that bet," Jackson said with a grin.

"Jesus," Ty muttered, shaking his head.

I grinned at my friends' obvious panic at the thought of marriage, even as I thought that I'd have no problem proposing to Natasha right this minute.

"All right, enough bachelor party talk," Jackson said, shooting me a grin. "Let's get down to what we all really want to know . . . What's up with Jericho and Natasha?"

I gave an exaggerated sigh and shook my head good-naturedly. Since Jackson's text, I'd been waiting for the conversation to shift.

"What's up with us, is that there *is* officially an *us*."

"I knew it," Jackson said.

"Good for you, man," Rob put in.

Mick nodded and tipped his beer at me, while Ty said, "I'm happy for you guys."

"Thanks," I replied. "It's been a long time coming, and I'm very happy and hopeful."

"I think all of this good news and shit calls for a round of shots," Mick said, standing up and looking around the table. "What say you, whiskey or tequila?"

There were a couple moans and some no thanks, but Mick just nodded and said, "Whiskey it is," and walked away.

"So, tomorrow's the big day, huh? You ready for Millie to move in?" Rob asked as Jackson passed out the beer.

"Very," Jackson replied. "Kayla made her a welcome home card and we've been cleaning and making room for Millie's things. We're having a big joint garage sale next weekend to get rid of any duplicate items, or things we don't need."

"Couldn't wait a few more weeks until after the wedding?" Ty joked.

"Heck no. At this point, the wedding is a formality to me. I mean, yeah, I'm looking forward to seeing Millie come down the aisle and for us to recite our vows, but in my heart, we've already made the commitment. You know what I mean, right, Jericho?" he asked me.

And, when I looked him in the eyes and nodded, I knew he read my intentions perfectly.

Natasha ~ Present

The last couple of weeks, Jericho and I had been working on finding our normal. We saw each other most nights, and fit in lunches, movie dates, or just met for a cup of coffee, whenever we could.

Prime Beef was still going strong and business at Three Sisters was booming. Since we were going to have a weekend off for Millie's bachelorette trip, we'd scheduled only a light load for our staff while we were away.

To make up for it, we had multiple events planned leading up to our mini-vacation.

After tons of applications and interviews, we'd decided to hire a well-qualified prior hotel catering manager to fill the new management position at Three Sisters. Tanisha Adams would be moving here from the city to take the position and was going to rent Millie's old apartment.

In fact, she was due to arrive at any moment, and we were busy trying to get her area finalized before her arrival. We'd rearranged our offices and brought in another desk to give Tanisha her own space in our growing world.

It was exciting how much we'd grown in so little time, but at the same time, I found it a bit overwhelming.

What had started as just my sisters and me had grown with a kitchen manager, and now an events and catering manager. Yes, it would be nice to free up a little time for us and to share some of the responsibility, but, at the same time, it was hard to hand over control to someone who wasn't *us*.

I was still going to do the accounting, but Tanisha would be taking over most of my other duties. As one of the owners, I'd still be involved and help with the planning and execution of events, but not as often as I had up until now.

It was strange, and my type A personality was already struggling with the transition.

"Tanisha is great. You saw her resume, spoke to her references, and said yourself upon meeting her that she'd fit in perfectly," Dru said when she caught me worrying my bottom lip.

"I know," I replied, then looked my sister in the eyes. "It's just that . . . everything's changing. And, yes, I know change is good, especially when it's because of how well Three Sisters is doing, it's just . . . hard for me to let go. Even a little bit."

"I know," Dru said, coming over to wrap her arms around my waist.

"But just think. This means we can take on more business, maybe work on that expansion we've been talking about . . . or, we can keep things as they are and have more free time for ourselves. You know Millie and Jackson are already talking babies, and when she gets pregnant, things will change even more. We'll be grateful for the ability to have that time for our personal lives."

I nodded, knowing she was right, but still, change had always been hard for me. I liked things to stay the same, to be in my control, and it seemed like in the last few months, everything had been constantly changing.

"It makes things like this bachelor/bachelorette trip possible," Dru added. "And, I have to say, I cannot wait to see the look on Jackson's face when he realizes that not only are we crashing their party, but the *freaking luxury travel van* Jericho rented is heading toward a literary adventure, rather than Vegas. He's going to shit a brick!"

I laughed at that.

"Nice image," I said wryly, wrinkling up my nose. "But yeah, you're right, he's going to be like a kid who just found out he's going to Disney World for the first time. I can't wait."

"And, although I hate to say anything nice about him, it's pretty freaking cool of Jericho to be funding this trip for all of us."

I sighed and shook my head with a small smile.

"I tried to tell him it was too much, that we could at least pay for our own lodging, but he wouldn't hear it. He said this group is like family and since he's never been able to have a family of his own to take care of, he was excited to be able to do something for all of us."

"Stop it, or you're going to make me start liking the guy," Dru joked softly.

But I turned to her and said seriously, "I really hope you will, because I think you were right . . . I still love him. I never stopped."

"Oh, baby girl, I know," Dru said, then gave me a kiss on the cheek before pulling away. "Enough of this mushy stuff, let's finish down here, then do one last check of the apartment to make sure everything is squared away."

Thirty minutes later we were through and ready for our new hire, just as she walked in the door.

"Hi," Dru greeted, stepping forward to shake Tanisha's hand.

"Welcome," I added. "Can we help you bring anything in?"

"Hi, and yes, that would be great. I only have a couple bags. My brother will be bringing up the rest of my things this weekend," Tanisha replied, shaking both of our hands then laughing. "I'm so excited to be here."

I smiled in return, her obvious pleasure at coming to Three Sisters easing some of my nerves.

We went out and helped her grab her bags from her car, then showed her up to Millie's . . . er, *her* apartment. It was furnished, although just with the basics, but it would be enough to get her by comfortably until her own things arrived.

"Wow, this is great," Tanisha said as she pushed her bag to the side and looked around. "It'll be so convenient to live right upstairs from work. No commute!"

Dru chuckled.

"Yes, being able to essentially roll out of bed and go to work is one of the best parts of living and working in the same building. I love my sleep."

Tanisha nodded, and asked, "So, Dru, you're right next door, and Natasha, you're at the end of the hall?"

"That's right," I replied. "We'll get out of your hair so you can get settled. Just holler if you need anything."

"Thanks so much."

Once we were out in the hall, Dru turned to me and said, "See, Tash, everything's going to work out just fine. Sometimes, change is a good thing."

I thought about all of the changes that had happened thus far, and realized she was right. We were all growing and changing for the better.

Jericho ~ Present

"No way! You cannot be serious! This is the best day ever!" Those were the phrases Jackson had been saying since we left town and found out that we weren't doing the guy's trip to Vegas, but the group literary trip.

The luxury van I'd booked was a smooth and comfortable ride. We'd taken turns driving, and Ty was now at the wheel. Jackson, Millie, Rob, and Dru were all sitting at the small table, playing cards as we cruised down the highway, while Natasha and I were laying on the bed in the back.

Fully clothed.

"Don't do anything freaky while you're five feet away from us," was what Dru had said when I'd led Natasha to the back a few moments ago.

I was no exhibitionist, so they really needn't worry, but Natasha had blushed just the same.

"Did I already mention how unbelievably sweet all of this was?" Natasha asked softly. We were both laying on our backs, staring out through the skylight, holding hands.

"Uh, yeah, about fifty times," I replied with a chuckle.

I was pleased she thought it was sweet, but I really didn't want anyone making a big deal out of it. Money was something I had plenty of, friends and family were not. I would have flown us all there in a private plane if necessary, but so far, I was really enjoying the road trip.

"Well, make it fifty-one," she said, turning her head toward me.

I shifted so I was looking at her as well, and said, "Noted."

"Are you excited about the trip?" Natasha asked.

"I'm excited to spend time with you."

She flushed prettily. "What about the museum, the fancy inn, and the book signing?"

I shrugged. "I'll get a kick out of watching Jackson, but I still don't even know who Nora Roberts is."

"She's a writer," Natasha began, a mocking smile on her lips. I didn't care if she was mocking me, I just liked the way she was looking at me. "She's written, like, a million books. Everything from contemporary romance, to fantasy, to romantic suspense, and she has a cool futuristic cop series under a pen name."

"So, she writes books, and opened a hotel and a bookstore?"

"Yeah, it's pretty cool. She even wrote it all into one of her series. The inn has different themed rooms based on the greatest literary couples. Jackson's not the only one who's going to be excited about that. Plus, I've always wanted to go to a real book signing."

"Hmmm, I didn't realize you'd enjoy this so much."

"Well, you don't know everything about me," Natasha mused, and I realized she was right, and that I was looking forward to learning these new facets of her, and all of the ways she'd changed since college.

"Yeah? Well, you don't know everything about me either," I

countered playfully.

"Oh, really?" she asked. "What surprises do you have in store for me?"

"For one," I whispered, "there's the way I can't stop thinking about you."

"What do you think about?"

"The things I want to do to you."

Her breath hitched.

"What things?"

I lifted my hand from hers to trace the swell of her lips.

"There's the way I want to taste you," I began, my voice low so only she could hear me. "Not here, but all over your body."

Her pupils dilated and she brushed her tongue across my thumb as she wet her lips.

"Where?" she asked, her tone rough with desire.

I kept my hands where they were, not wanting to make everyone else suspicious about our conversation, but raked my eyes down her body.

"First I'd kiss that spot where you neck meets your shoulder. Lick it. Suck it. Then, I'd move down to your breasts, where your nipples are puckered, waiting, eager for the heat of my mouth. I'd spend a great deal of time there, loving first one breast, then the other. Taking your nipples between my lips. Between my teeth."

Natasha gasped and shifted on the bed.

"I'd lick a trail down your stomach, over your hips, until I reached the place where you're aching for me right now. You *are* aching for me, aren't you, Natasha?"

"*Yes*," she practically moaned, the sound making me shift on the bed as well.

"Then, I'd place my mouth . . ."

"Oh my God, we're here!" Jackson shouted, and I didn't bother biting back my groan as he jumped up out of his seat. "The Emily Dickinson Museum!"

I shifted my gaze to Natasha, then grinned when I saw her glaring back at me.

"I'm going to kill you for this," she whispered.

I chuckled and said, "I look forward to it," then stood up and offered her my hand.

She reluctantly gave it to me. I helped her to her feet and we followed the rest of the group off of the van.

"Hey," Dru said, coming up to us and throwing her arm around Natasha's shoulder. "I said no freaky business on the bus."

Dru looked pointedly at Natasha's flushed cheeks, then back at me and gave me a glare identical to the one Natasha was still giving me.

"What?" I asked, holding up my hands in surrender. "I didn't touch her . . . promise."

With that said, I shot them a wink and a grin, tipped my imaginary hat, and sauntered off to watch Jackson geek out over the Emily Dickinson Museum.

Twenty-Five

Natasha ~ Present

*T*he Emily Dickinson Museum had been great. Very informative and cool to see, and watching Jackson positively swoon as he meandered through was the icing on the cake.

We drove a little more after our tour was over, eager to be on our way to Boonsboro, Maryland, but ended up agreeing to stop for the night. We'd done a lot of traveling, and although the van was a luxury, we decided sitting down to a nice dinner and sleeping in a hotel would be best. That way we could wake up and be refreshed, ready to finish the drive and explore Nora's town.

We'd found a hotel with a restaurant and bar inside on the map and made our way to it. Before we'd even arrived, Jericho had already called, secured four rooms, and paid for all of them.

"You know we could have paid for our own rooms tonight. You've already done so much," I'd whispered to Jericho as we exited the van, grabbed our bags, and followed the others inside.

"It's no big deal. I said I'd cover the trip, and this is still part of it. The money's just sitting there, not being used," Jericho said, his face sharing his exasperation.

I knew he was probably getting tired of me talking about it, but . . ."I don't want you to feel like we're using you for your money. That's all."

"Hey," Jericho called softly, pulling me to him so I was facing him, his arm coming around me. "I know you guys wouldn't do that, okay . . . and, this was all my idea, so quit worrying about it."

I nodded, then let my eyelids flutter shut when he bent to kiss me.

"Now, no more talk of money. Promise?" he asked, his breath warm against my lips.

"Promise," I vowed, opening my eyes and smiling up at him. "Let's go put our bags in the room and find that restaurant, I'm starving."

"You got it."

It looked like everyone had the same idea, so we agreed to meet back downstairs in five minutes and go to dinner. While in the elevator, Jericho called ahead to let the restaurant know that a party of seven was headed there way.

"This is nice," I said when he opened the door to reveal a contemporary-style room with a king-sized bed. It wasn't big or elaborate, but it was clean and the bed looked inviting.

"It's a room," Jericho said with a shrug, unimpressed. Right then, my stomach growled loudly, causing us both to laugh. "Let's get you down to dinner."

When we stepped off the elevator, Rob, Ty, and Dru were standing off to the side talking. As we drew near, I could hear them say Jackson and Millie's names.

"What's up?" I asked as we approached.

Dru looked over at me and wiggled her eyebrows.

"Jackson and Millie won't be joining us, they're ordering in."

"Can't say I blame them," Jericho said roughly in my ear, then more loudly to the group, "Let's go on in then, we can tell the hostess when we arrive that we'll be two less."

Once we were seated, placed our orders, and our drinks arrived, I felt like I could finally sit back and relax. Enjoy a moment of calm in a day that had been full of *go, go, go*. I leaned back in my chair and sipped my wine as I listened to Rob and Ty go back and forth about who drove the van better.

"You have to admit, my lane transitions were totally smooth," Ty said.

"True, but did you see the way I handled *The Beast* when that Rav 4 cut in front of me?" Rob asked.

They'd started calling the luxury van *The Beast* around mile ten.

"Tomorrow, I'm driving," Dru informed us, causing everyone to groan in response. Even me.

Dru scowled and asked, "*What?*"

I loved my sister, truly, but Dru was a terrible driver. The worst. Anytime I got in the car with her I said a prayer and held on for dear life. I don't know why she was so bad, she'd learned from our mom, just like Millie and I had, and had the same Driver's Ed teacher. She just never got the hang of it.

"Didn't I hear that you once drove straight into a row of shopping carts? Not backed into, but hit them head on?" Rob asked, leaning on the table as he grinned at Dru, who looked like she wanted to kick him.

"And, what about the time you literally hit a chicken that was crossing the road?" Ty added.

"Did you guys hear about the time when she gunned it through a light after it had turned red, and totaled the car?" I asked, and this time Dru *did* kick me under the table.

"Ow!" I cried, frowning at her.

"Good thing it's not up to any of you. Jericho is the one who rented the van, so he can decide if I can drive it or not."

Dru looked at Jericho expectantly, her expression daring him to deny her.

He opened his mouth, then shut it again, and I knew he was conflicted because he was doing his best to make Dru like him, but he wanted us to arrive at Nora's Inn in one piece.

Knowing I needed to save him from her wrath, I turned to my sister and said, "Dru, you don't even have a license right now. It's still suspended, remember? You can't drive on a suspended license. If you got caught, Jericho could get in trouble with the rental agency and you'd get more than a slap on the wrist this time."

Dru pursed her lips, then nodded reluctantly and agreed, "I guess you're right. I don't want to get Jericho in trouble."

The table let out a collective sigh of relief, then laughed when Dru shot daggers at all of us.

"Thanks, babe," Jericho whispered, and I squeezed his hand under the table.

"Anytime."

Twenty-Six

Jericho ~ Present

J shifted on the bed, my body warming automatically as I brushed up against Natasha. I opened my eyes, giving myself a moment to adjust to the low light in the room, then drank in the sight of her sleeping face.

I felt more at peace in that moment than I probably had in my entire life.

Her red hair was falling over her forehead, and half covering her eye. Her face was turned toward me, and her lips were tipped up, indicating she was at peace as well, or at least having a good dream.

I slipped an arm around her waist, snuggling in closer and closing my eyes as I let her scent surround me and the soft planes of her body fit against me. She sighed and moved, and I stilled, not wanting to wake her.

The past few weeks had been like a dream to me.

Nothing like college, or the relationship we'd had before. No, now we were two grown adults with our own businesses, our own lives, making it work as a functioning couple. Did we get to see each other every day? No, not always, but I made it a point to send her texts, notes, or call, to let her know I was thinking of her.

With the way things were going, I knew they'd only get better, because eventually, we would live together, so we would see each other every day. Then marriage, and a family. It was everything I'd ever wanted, and had been too afraid to hope for.

I knew Natasha still had doubts, stemming mostly from her father's abandonment of his family, but I hoped, I'd proven, not just recently, but with my commitment to her even over the years we were apart, that I was nothing like her father.

"Jericho," she whispered, and I opened my eyes to see her face a few inches from me. She was smiling, all warm and sleepily, and I had no choice but to brush my lips against hers.

"Go back to sleep," I replied softly. "It's still early."

I felt her hand come up between us, then she ran her thumb gently over my cheek.

"I love you," she said, and just like that I was whole.

I moved us until Natasha was on her back, and settled between her legs. I ran my hand over her hair, caressed her face, and lowered my head to cover her lips with mine. After I kissed us both breathless, I brought my head up so that I could look her in the eyes.

"I love you, too," I replied. "I never stopped."

"Me neither," she admitted softly. "As much as I tried, it was impossible. I'll love you forever."

We'd come together in a frenzy after dinner and drinks with our friends, eager for one another after the teasing in the van. We'd fallen asleep naked, which made me very, very happy in that moment.

I moved down slightly, taking her nipple in my mouth as I simultaneously rubbed the hard, weeping head of my cock against her opening, then slid up to tease her clit. She opened for me, her legs falling to the side as she arched, giving me better access to her breasts.

"*Jericho*," Natasha moaned, and I could feel her body responding to me, becoming wetter with each stroke.

She tilted her hips up, grinding against me as I thrust into her. I slid inside, slowly, enjoying every inch, until I was seated fully inside of her. Releasing her breast, I kissed my way back up to her mouth, then paused, a breath away from claiming her lips.

"I love you, Natasha," I said again, then I took her lips as I began to move.

Our hands found each other and entwined as her legs came around my waist. We made love with soft sounds, sighs, and whispers, worshiping each other with our mouths and hearts as we came together as one.

Spent from one of the most precious experiences of my life, I rested my forehead on hers as we struggled to calm our labored breathing.

Once the feeling started to come back into my limbs, I moved off of her, not wanting to crush her, pulling her with me so that she was sprawled across me. One hand at her back, the other caressing her arm, as she left sweet kisses on my chest.

I was about to tell her how amazing she was, when her stomach interrupted my thoughts.

"Are you hungry again?" I asked with a chuckle.

Natasha blushed prettily and bent her head to bite my skin gently.

"Do you blame me?" she asked. "Aren't you hungry?"

"What time is it?"

She shifted to look over her shoulder, giving me a perfect view of her lightly tanned torso and gorgeous breasts.

"Almost six," Natasha replied, looking back and catching me in the act.

I grinned unabashedly and said, "I could eat, but first, I think we need to wash up. I for one am feeling very dirty."

Natasha raised an eyebrow and asked, "Again?"

"Always."

I grabbed her close and swung my feet to the floor, lifting her with me as I rose, smiling when her light, happy laugh filled the room.

I managed to get us both into the bathroom and turned on the shower without injuring either of us, then proceeded to show her just how dirty I was feeling, and did my best to clean us both up.

By the time we made it downstairs, the rest of our group was already enjoying breakfast. They looked up as we approached, taking in our wet hair, freshly scrubbed skin, and what I was sure were matching satisfied faces.

I just smiled at the lot of them and said, "What's good? We're starved."

Twenty-Seven

Natasha ~ Present

"We'll be serving complimentary wine and cheese from six to seven this evening, and complimentary breakfast in the morning. We have a lounge, library, dining room, and patio, feel free to use any of the common areas throughout the day. You can also use your room key to gain access to Fit In Boonsboro, to utilize their fitness equipment, steam room, or sauna. If you have any questions, don't hesitate to ask, and we hope you enjoy your stay here at Inn Boonsboro."

We'd finally reached our destination and had checked into the inn. Jackson was practically writhing with excitement, like a puppy who wanted to explore. The plan was to check into our rooms, then head out as a group to discover the town.

The book signing wasn't until tomorrow, so the evening was ours. All I could say was that I was happy to be out of *The Beast*, and ready to stretch my legs and see what the quaint town of Boonsboro had to offer.

"Jackson and Millie, you'll be in the Elizabeth and Darcy room," the innkeeper continued, biting back a smile at Jackson's excited squeak. "Jericho and Natasha, you have Eve and Roarke. Rob and Ty, Marguerite and Percy. And, last, but not least, Drusilla, Titania and Oberon."

"It's just Dru," Dru said. She really hated when people called her Drusilla.

"Sorry," the innkeeper replied easily. "Dru. Please, follow me, and I'll show you to your rooms."

As we walked through the inn, my head swiveled as I tried to take it all in. The reception area and lobby were both beautiful, with exposed brick and a fireplace crackling as we walked past.

We stopped at a door downstairs, "Marguerite and Percy," and when Rob and Ty walked inside, I tried to get a good look, but all I saw were two full beds, before we were moving to the stairs to go up.

When we got to Titania and Oberon, I couldn't stop myself from going inside with Dru. I had to see what it looked like.

"Oh my gosh!" Dru cried when she saw the beautiful canopy bed, the door leading out to the terrace, and then the deep copper tub in the bathroom. "This is the prettiest room I've ever seen. I'm never leaving."

I laughed as she laid back onto the bed and moved her arms like she was making a snow angel.

"It's so beautiful," I agreed, looking around to take it all in.

"Let's go see ours," I heard Jackson say, turning to see him walking out of Dru's room, intent on finding his Elizabeth and Darcy room.

I chuckled and followed him out to see Jericho waiting for me with a smile.

"I think she likes it," I told him as I took his hand in mine, grateful that he'd been so thoughtful to get her a special room like that, especially when she was the only one sleeping alone.

Well, not that Ty and Rob were sleeping together, but, they were best buds, and although she had me and Millie, I wished she had someone like we did to make her happy.

"Seems that way," Jericho replied.

"And, here you are," the innkeeper said as she led us to our room.

As we entered, I could hear Jackson exclaiming over his own room. The Eve and Roarke room was a mixture of clean, modern lines and antique furnishes, with a cool chair in the corner. As I was walking through it, I heard Jericho call, "Come see this," from the bathroom, so I followed him inside.

It was gorgeous, with a state-of-the-art shower built for two, and a free-standing tub that begged me to relax with a good book.

"Oh, I love these robes," I said, stroking my hand down the soft sleeve of one of the hanging robes.

"This place is pretty cool. Rob and Ty did good," Jericho said.

I walked over and placed my arms around his waist to look up at him and clarify, "*You* did good."

He took my lips with his and we got lost in each other for a few seconds, before he pulled back, then dropped another couple quick kisses on my lips.

"Ready to go out and explore?" he asked.

"You bet," I replied, hugging his waist briefly before letting him go.

We left our bags on the bed and headed back downstairs to see if anyone else was ready. When we arrived, everyone but Dru was already waiting.

"Hey," Jackson said, crossing to us as we hit the landing. "How was your room? I wanted to come see it, but Millie said I should give you guys some privacy. Can I see it later?"

"Sure, but only if I can see yours," I replied with a laugh.

"Deal," Jackson said, totally serious. "So, I was thinking, we could hit Main Street, check out the shops and stuff. Then, come back here at six for the wine and cheese, before heading to Dan's Restaurant and Taphouse for dinner. What do you think?"

The five of us looked at each other, then back and Jackson. "Whatever you want, man, it's your party," Jericho answered for the group.

"Well, it's Millie's party, too," he said, turning to his fiancée. "What do you think, Mills?"

"Sounds perfect," my sister said, looking up at him with an expression of utter devotion.

"Hey, sorry, guys, I got sidetracked in my kick-ass room," Dru called as she came down the stairs. Her voice sounded cheery, which had me looking at her more closely. Not that Dru couldn't be cheery, she could, there just seemed to be an edge to it.

Although she had a smile on her face that seemed genuine, I noticed that she was clutching her phone hard enough for her knuckles to turn white.

"No problem," Jackson said, shooting her a face-splitting smile, oblivious to any signs of distress. "Let's do this."

Vowing to check in with her later, I followed my soon-to-be brother-in-law out onto the street.

Twenty-Eight

Jericho ~ Present

We were on our way home.

The trip had been a success. Everyone had a good time. We didn't have any arguments or differences of opinion on what to do or where to go, which was often the case with large groups. I think because we'd all known from the get-go that this was Jackson's dream trip, and we were all just along for the ride.

I was actually surprised by how much fun I'd had, a literary trip never having crossed my mind as something I'd ever be interested in.

But, there was something to be said about traveling and discovering new things with a great group of people. That's what made all the difference. Sure, there were moments when Jackson missed Kayla and wondered if he should have brought her along, but he bought her a trinket at every stop to let her know he'd been thinking of her.

We'd all met Nora Roberts, who was a friendly woman, and had made Jackson's day when she took a picture with him and told him to keep doing great work with his students.

Natasha had gotten her signed book and had gotten a little star struck as well.

Now, we were driving back home, hoping to make it back before too late, since all of us had to be back to work in the morning. Jackson and Millie were snoozing on the bed in the back, while Natasha and Dru were laying down on the table that converted into a bed. Rob was driving *The Beast* with Ty in the passenger seat and I'd been catching up on emails and checking Prime Beef's social media accounts.

When my phone started ringing in my hand, startling me, I quickly turned it to silent so as not to wake anyone up. The number wasn't familiar, but thinking it could be something about the restaurant, I answered as quietly as I could.

"Ric, you're a hard boy to track down. How are you doing, son?"

The voice on the other end had my blood turning cold. I stood swiftly, looking around the small space as I tried to find somewhere I could get a modicum of privacy. My gaze settled on the bathroom door and I made it there in four quick steps, then shut myself inside.

"How did you get this number?" I asked harshly.

My mother chuckled and replied, "I think you'll remember that I'm like a dog with a bone when I want something. It took a couple weeks, but I eventually found your trail of breadcrumbs."

I was about to retort, when I realized something, "This isn't a collect call . . ."

"Nope, I got out. Good behavior."

Fuck. Good behavior, my ass.

"And, I was thinking it's high time I saw my boy, what since you haven't once come to visit me in all these years."

"I'd think you'd pick up those clues and realize it's because I don't want anything to do with you. When you left me to fend for myself, more worried about your next fix than taking care of your son, you made that decision pretty easy."

"Oh, come on now, Ric, people change, you know that. Hell, look at you. *My* boy, from the streets of Philly to running his own restaurant, and richer than God himself."

"Ah, I see, this isn't about seeing me . . . it's about the money. That's what this is," I said, my breath leaving me in a rush. At least now I knew her motive for calling me. Fuck if she was going to get a dime from me.

"Sure, I heard about it, how else would my son be able to pay for college and get his shit cleaned up enough to find himself a pretty, privileged white piece of ass to stick it to."

"I'm hanging up," I said, my blood boiling even as I felt a cold sweat hit. I never thought I'd hear her voice again, let alone have to listen to her mouth. I was sure she'd be dead by now, either from drugs or prison.

"Not before we set up a time to meet, Ric. I want to see my boy, and we need to talk about that money. See, I ain't got no job, and although I've been crashing on a couple couches, I sure could use a place of my own."

"Fuck that. I don't want to see you, and you aren't getting shit from me."

"It's a boy's job to take care of his mother."

"I took care of you enough when I was too young to take care of myself. I want nothing to do with you, you need to figure shit out for yourself."

"Listen here, *Jericho Roger Smythe*, your daddy took all my good years then disappeared without so much as a *fuck you*. No child support or nothin', leaving me with our son and no way to live. The way I see it, that money's just as much mine as yours, if not more. So, I'm coming to see you, and if you want me to leave you alone, you best have my check ready when I do."

"If I see you on my property, I'll have you arrested for trespassing, and I'm not giving you a goddamned thing. If you know what's good for you, you'll forget I exist and get on with your miserable life."

"I'll be seeing you," my mother promised, then hung up the phone.

"*Fuck*," I whispered, looking blindly around the small bathroom and wanting to hit something, to break something so bad that it took every ounce of my control to keep my fists at my side.

My mind raced as I wondered what my next move would be. The last thing I needed was my mother coming here and ruining everything I'd worked so hard to build. And, I didn't want her toxicity touching Natasha.

I couldn't let it happen.

I lifted my hand with my phone and searched my contacts, then hit call.

When the gruff voice greeted me on the other line, I said quickly, "Mick, I need your help."

Twenty-Nine

Natasha ~ Present

I was at my desk, going through the event book, double checking it against the accounts, and trying to finalize our schedule for the next three months. It was a few days since we'd come back from our trip, and I still felt like I was playing catch up.

Tanisha was great, but I was still getting used to her presence, both professionally and personally.

Millie was giving Claire more of the workload in the kitchen as her wedding date drew near, and with her living at Jackson's, I felt like I hardly got to see her.

Both Dru and Jericho were just acting . . . off.

I'd tried talking to Dru about what had happened at the inn, but she'd just waved me off and changed the subject.

And, Jericho? He'd been distant.

No, I didn't expect him to spend every waking second with me. In fact, I'd been the one talking about how we needed to still live our lives, but, since we'd come home, I hadn't even seen him. Not once.

I was trying really hard not to freak out.

We still texted, and talked on the phone. But he hadn't spent the night, or invited me to do so at his house. Sure, I probably could have taken it upon myself to go to his house and invite myself to spend the night, but I found his distance was making me question things.

Plus, I'd gotten sick after we came home, and had been fighting dizziness and fatigue.

All in all, things currently sucked, and trying to distract myself with work wasn't helping. Maybe I needed to take over an event, or go help Claire in the kitchen. I was no chef, but I followed directions really well.

I stood up, eager to take a minute away from my desk, when another wave of dizziness had me sitting back down.

"You okay?" Tanisha asked as she stepped into the room.

Millie was off today, and Dru was out doing God knows what, so it was just Tanisha and me in the office.

"Uh, yeah," I said, waving my hand to indicate it was no big deal. "Just too many hours at this desk with no food. I was thinking of walking down to Rooster's to get some tea and a muffin or something. Do you want anything?"

Tanisha walked over and sat down across from my desk. She looked fabulous in a bright-red suit jacket and A-line skirt, her dark braids pulled back and secured at her neck.

"Still feeling . . . *off*?" she asked gently, her dark eyes probing.

"Yeah, nothing a little food and shut-eye won't fix," I replied with a shrug.

"Natasha, is there any possibility you could be pregnant?" Tanisha asked, and my eyes flew to her face in shock as I lost all feeling in my body.

"What? No, I mean, yes . . . but, I'm on the pill," I said desperately, my mind reeling.

"Birth control isn't a hundred percent. Have you missed a day here and there? The only reason I ask is that's what happened to me, and your symptoms look the same."

"I didn't know you had a child," I managed, even though I was trying to remember everything I'd done over the past weeks.

"I don't," she replied sadly. I looked up and focused on her for a second. "I actually lost the baby about six months ago. That's part of the reason I moved here and changed jobs, I needed to get away from the memories. Start fresh."

"I'm so sorry," then asked, curious, even though I didn't want to pry, "And, the father?"

"He's moved on as well, although he's still back in the city. Anyway, I didn't tell you that to make this about me . . ."

"The first time," I muttered once my mind finally finished cataloging events. "With Jericho . . . It had been years so I wasn't on anything. And, we didn't . . . I started the pills again after the first time."

I think she saw the panic setting in, because she said, "Why don't you go and get a test and find out for sure, before you get yourself worked up. It could be just a bug."

I nodded, although now that she'd put the thought in my head, the more it made sense.

Oh my God, what am I going to do?

"Hey," Tanisha said, standing and coming around my desk to place her hand on my shoulder.

I stood and accepted the comfort she offered.

"Get the test first," she said again, and I nodded against her shoulder. "No matter what happens, you have a great support system. Your sisters, Jericho, and I'm happy to help in any way I can."

Jericho. What is he going to think about all of this?

"Test," I said aloud, telling myself not to worry until I knew I had something to worry about. Tanisha was right, I did have a great support system. I'd be fine and figure out what to do once I knew the results.

Still, as I walked toward the door, my body felt completely numb.

"Do you want me to come with you, or call one of your sisters?" Tanisha offered.

"Could you?" I asked gratefully. "Can you come with me, and ask them to meet us at my apartment?"

"Sure can," she said, and started calling as we walked out the back door and headed toward the pharmacy.

"Hey, Millie, yes, it's Tanisha. Do you think you can meet us at Natasha's apartment in thirty minutes? No, nothing is wrong, she just needs a . . . family meeting. Thanks."

I listened as if through a tunnel as she made the same call to Dru. Once we reached the pharmacy, I stood in the street, staring at the door, but unable to put one foot in front of the other and go inside.

"Do you want me to get one?" Tanisha asked.

"Yeah, or two . . . maybe five," I replied.

Tanisha chuckled and said, "You got it."

I stayed there, standing on the sidewalk in front of the store, half afraid I'd find out I was pregnant, and half afraid I wouldn't.

Thirty

Jericho ~ Present

*A*ny other time I would have kicked back, had a beer, and enjoyed the cool vibe of Mick's office / man cave.

Today, all I could think about was finding my mother and keeping her away from everything I held dear.

"Nothing?" I asked Mick from one of his plush leather chairs.

"Not yet, man, but I've only just begun. Don't worry, I'll find her," my friend assured me. "Last known address, Riverside Correctional Facility. I've been in contact and have the name of her parole officer, who said she hasn't missed a visit yet. He gave me the address for the halfway house she listed as her residence, but if what she told you is correct, and she's bunking with old friends, she'll be a little harder to track."

"Old friends?" I scoffed. "She's burned every bridge she ever had. More than likely, she's bunking with new clients, or strangers she meets while looking for her next fix."

"I've got a recent photo, and, man, she looks like she's put some miles in; you wanna see it?"

"No," I replied curtly. Certainly not mad at Mick, but pissed about having to deal with this situation at all.

"Got it. Okay, I'm leaving for Philly right after this, so if you think of anything else pertinent, text me."

"All right, and seriously, man, thanks again."

"You can thank me once I find her and serve the restraining order," Mick replied, then stood up behind his desk. "I'll keep you up to date on my progress. Let me know if she contacts you again."

"Will do," I said, rising as well and sticking out my hand. "Thanks again, it means a lot."

Mick just nodded and I saw myself out.

I'd spent the week getting information to Mick and working on getting the restraining order. Between the shit with my mom and dealing with the restaurant, I'd gotten home late each night and had fallen into bed exhausted, only to average three hours of sleep a night.

I hadn't seen Natasha since I'd dropped her off in *The Beast* after our trip. I'd called and texted her, but I knew if she saw me, she'd know something was up, and I was so fucking embarrassed about my mother.

I didn't want any of this shit to touch her.

Still, I missed her, and I didn't know how long I'd be able to keep her at arm's length. I could tell by her tone that she was getting frustrated and maybe a little hurt, but I felt like I was stuck between a rock and a hard place, and I didn't know what to do.

"How come you're dealing with this shit on your own? Where's Natasha? Did she bail at the first sign of trouble?" Hector had asked last night when he stopped by my office at eleven at night after closing down the kitchen.

"Watch it," I'd warned him, too exhausted and pissed to put up with his shit. "She doesn't know anything about it."

"You didn't tell her?" my friend asked with a frown. When I shook my head, he said, "How are you going to move forward with this relationship if you're not being honest? Do you think she can't handle it? Do you think she'll run?"

"No, it's not that, it's just, you know my ma . . . She's a hot mess. Everything she touches turns to shit. I don't want her anywhere near Natasha. She doesn't get to ruin any other part of my life," I said, dropping my head in my hands with a frustrated groan.

"I understand your mom's a piece of work, but you've talked to the cops and Mick is gonna handle it. If you don't let Natasha be there for you when you need her the most, you're doing her, and your relationship, a disservice."

"Oh, now you want me to make the relationship work?" I asked sarcastically, my bad mood making me an asshole.

Hector shook his head and crossed his arms, unaffected by my nastiness.

"I'm not convinced yet, but if *you* are, then you need to let her in. If she's the woman you say she is, she won't want to be protected or coddled from your life, she'll want to be there by your side. At least, that's what I *hope* will happen . . . for your sake."

He'd left me then, alone in my misery, but I hadn't gone to her last night, or this morning.

Now that Mick was on his way to Philly to serve my mother the papers, and things would hopefully get resolved, I realized Hector was right. I *was* doing Natasha a disservice by keeping her in the dark.

She already knew about my mother, our past . . . my history, and it had never changed the way she saw me.

I just hoped she wouldn't be pissed that I hadn't told her as soon as my mom had phoned me. Lord knew, *I* would be if something like this was happening in her life, and she hadn't told me about it. Let me help her.

"*Shit*," I muttered as I turned my car toward Main Street. I *was* an asshole.

As I was about to pick up my phone and dial Natasha, it rang.

"Millie? What's up?" I asked as I answered, since I'd never gotten a phone call from Millie before. I hadn't even realized I had her programed into my phone.

Natasha must have done it . . .

"Can you come by Natasha's apartment?" she asked, her tone not cause for alarm, but still I had to ask, "Is everything okay?"

"Yeah, it's fine, I just think you should be here. Hurry?"

"Be there in three minutes," I replied, wondering what was going on now.

Thirty-One

Natasha ~ Present

I was still in the bathroom.

I'd heard Millie arrive, then Dru, but I hadn't yet come out of my cocoon.

As long as I stayed in, and kept the results to myself, then they weren't a living, breathing truth that I had to deal with.

But, then I heard another knock on the door, this one kind of frantic, and heard Jericho come into my apartment. That's when I stood and crossed to the door and swung it wide open.

I probably looked a bit crazy, standing in the doorway holding a pregnancy test in my fist like a lifeline, a stick I'd peed on only a little while earlier. But then, I was *feeling* a bit crazy, after all, I'd just been smacked in the face with another major life change.

"Hey, what's going . . ." Jericho's eyes locked on my hand. "Is that what I . . . ?"

Before he could get it out, I ran at him full speed. Past my sisters' shocked faces, and Tanisha's smiling face, right into Jericho's arms.

I was crying and babbling, not really sure what to say or do, but needing his comfort.

"Oh my God, we're having a baby. We only just found each other again, and said we were going to try and take things slow . . . get used to being in each other's lives again. But that first night, after Millie's engagement party, when you followed me here, and we, and we didn't . . . it happened. Holy crap, this is really happening."

I took a deep breath and was about to go on another rant, when I felt myself being spun around and the sound of Jericho's happy laughter registered.

I picked my head up off of his chest and looked up into his smiling face.

"You're pregnant?" he asked, his voice overflowing with joy.

I nodded, still in shock, then held out the stick that was clutched in my hand.

"According to this stick, and the four others in the bathroom, yes, I'm pregnant. But, I think we can't say it's a hundred percent until we go to the doctor."

"Okay," Jericho began, his expression changing to his *all business* face. "First, we will make you an appointment and make sure you're all good, then, we'll pack up your stuff and move you out to my place . . . I mean, our place. Once you're all settled, we can start talking wedding plans."

"Whoa, easy there," I choked, pushing free of his arms and standing firmly on my feet again. "We don't even know *for sure* that I'm pregnant and you're already hearing wedding bells."

"Natasha," Jericho said, bending to take my face in his palms. "They're usually pretty accurate, and I don't want to miss a minute of this pregnancy. If you want me to move into your apartment here, I will, although I think we'd be more comfortable in our house. I want to be there if you're sick, get you the things you crave, rub your feet and your back, anything you need. I want to experience everything in a way that I wouldn't be able to if we stay apart."

I was listening, and although I felt slightly nauseous, what he was saying made sense.

"Tasha, I'm going to marry you, and we're going to live together. We love each other, and we've agreed that we want to stay together and really make this work, so let's do this. Move in with me. Marry me. Pregnant or not, I want this. I want you."

I let out a gush of breath with a short laugh.

"Are you really proposing right now?" I asked incredulously, thinking this day had turned out so much different than expected.

"Well, I don't have a ring, and I know I can give you a much better proposal with a little more time, but *yes*, consider this the precursor to the proposal," Jericho said, taking my hand in his.

My heart was pounding, and I felt like I might faint, but I looked into his eyes and said, "Yes, I'll move in with you, but you don't get your answer to the proposal until it happens."

"Fair enough," he said, then took me into his arms and kissed me.

I heard cheers and clapping and realized I'd forgotten about our audience. Once Jericho broke the kiss, I turned to my sisters and let out a squeal.

"Whoa, we're going to be aunties," Dru said excitedly as they rushed toward me.

"Oh, Natasha, I'm so happy for you," Millie said, her arms coming around me as she pulled me close.

"I can't believe it," I cried, because even though I said I needed the official confirmation from a doctor, I knew it instinctively that I was pregnant. "I'm going to be someone's mom."

"You're going to be terrific at it," Dru said, and I reached over to pull her in for a hug. When I let her go, she turned to Jericho and added, "I guess this means we're in it together for the long haul."

"I guess it does," Jericho said somewhat warily, shooting me a startled glance when Dru gave him a quick hug, then backed away.

"Well, I for one am ecstatic, welcome to the family," Millie said, hugging him as well.

"Jeez, let's not get ahead of ourselves," I said with a chuckle. "Let me get used to one thing at a time. *Please.*"

"She's never been big on change," Millie told Jericho, as if I weren't still standing right next to them.

"This, I know," Jericho replied, causing me to glare at them both.

"Just for that, you guys are packing and moving all of my stuff," I told them.

"What stuff?" Millie asked jokingly. "My apartment had more in it when it was empty than yours does right now."

"As if I'd let you lift a finger in your condition," Jericho added with a wink.

I stuck my tongue out at Millie and rolled my eyes at Jericho.

"Whatever," I said then turned to Dru. "Hey, favorite sister, what do you say you take me downstairs and help me find some food for my belly while I find a doctor?"

"Ohhh, favorite sister, I like that," Dru said, also sticking her tongue out at Millie, who was pouting prettily.

"I want to come, too," Millie complained.

"Oh, fine, you can both come, but no more ganging up on me with Jericho. Sisters stick together, no matter what."

Jericho kissed me on the cheek and said, "Let me know what the doctor says and when our appointment is, in the meantime, I'll find a moving company and get it set up. But, hey, I'd love it if you'd pack a bag and meet me at home tonight."

"Sounds good," I replied, then went in search of some nourishment for me and our baby.

Thirty-Two

Jericho ~ Present

"I picked up this dresser today, and moved all of my stuff to one side of the closet. Plus, I cleared out some drawers and counter space in the bathroom. If you need any more room, or *anything* else, just let me know and I'll make it happen."

We'd wheeled Natasha's suitcases into the bedroom, and I had her overnight bag slung over my shoulder. In reality, with her clothes, shoes, and toiletries packed, there wasn't a whole lot more for the movers to bring over.

"Wow, you did all of this today?" Natasha asked, sticking her head in the closet then looking back at me in wonder. "That's incredibly sweet."

"I want you to feel at home," I replied, setting her bag on the bed. "Do you want to put stuff away first, or eat first?"

"Eat, definitely," she said, patting her flat belly, and as I looked down at her hand, I imagined what she'd look like once a few months had passed and she was starting to show.

I can't wait.

"Then let's go get cooking." I held my elbow out gallantly, and she tucked her hand inside with a smile.

In the kitchen, I had the makings for chicken stir fry and rice, one of the first meals we'd ever made together back in my old apartment. Natasha looked at me, her eyes slightly misty, then tucked into me and gave me a hug.

Then we got to work.

It was just like when we were younger. I put on the rice, while Natasha started chopping, then we worked seamlessly together until the stir fry was plated and we were ready to share our first meal together in *our* home.

"Do you want water, juice, or maybe some ginger ale?" I asked as I pulled out a water for myself.

"Um, water sounds good," Natasha said, then looked at the bottle in my hand and added, "You know, you can have a beer, or whatever you want. Just cause I'm not drinking doesn't mean you can't."

"Nah, like I said, I want to experience everything about this pregnancy with you. That means, no drinking until you can."

"Does that mean you're going to puke when I puke, too?" she asked with a grin as we sat at the table.

"No, smart ass, but I want to support you and *really* do this with you."

"Sweet," Natasha said again, with a shake of her head then took her first bite of stir fry. "Mmmmm, so good."

"Yeah?" I asked with a chuckle, pleased that we still had it. As if it were a test that we'd needed to pass and had.

Natasha nodded, and as I joined her in eating, I knew it was time to fill her in on what was going on with my mother.

"You know how I've been busy since we got back?"

"Yeah," Natasha replied, hovering her hand over her mouth

when she talked.

"When we were driving back from Maryland, I got a call from my mother."

Natasha put down her fork and reached for my hand.

"She's out of jail, has been for a few weeks, and I guess she's been looking for me. She heard about the money from my grandfather, and is looking for a cut. She threatened to come here, but Mick left this morning for Philly. He's gonna find her and serve her papers, plus tell her she's not getting a dime."

"That's awful, I'm so sorry. I can't believe it's the first time she's talked to you in all this time, and all she's worried about is money. Why didn't you tell me?" Natasha asked. Not angrily, just curious.

"At first, I was embarrassed. That she's my mother and as you said, couldn't care less about reconnecting with me, just concerned about getting money. I think I'm also not used to coming to you with stuff yet. It's not that things haven't been going great, they have . . . And it's not that I thought you'd get scared and not stand by me. It's more that I'm used to Hector being my sounding board now, and, although I don't want that to change, you should be the first person I come to when something is going wrong. Or, right, for that matter."

Natasha squeezed my hand and nodded.

"I get it, truly I do. I'm so used to my sisters being my first call whenever anything happens, that it almost doesn't feel real until I've talked to them. But I promise the same, you'll be my first call from now on."

"It's a pact," I agreed, running my thumb over her hand before releasing it so we could both resume eating. "How are you feeling?"

"Great. I mean, I get nauseous sometimes, but when I eat a little something I feel better. I think my body's telling me to snack more in between meals, rather than getting stuck at my desk and going long stretches of no eating."

"Maybe keeping some nuts and string cheese or something at your desk will help."

"Yeah, I'll grab some stuff tomorrow . . . It still seems so surreal. I know I said we had to wait to hear it from the doctor, but I'm ninety-nine percent sure that I'm pregnant. I can hardly believe it."

"And, does that make you happy?" I asked, hopeful that she was as ecstatic as I was.

Her smile was gorgeous when she replied, "Yes. Very happy. And, I take it from your reaction earlier, that you're happy, too?"

"Thrilled," I assured her. "This baby is going to have two parents that love him or her and will do everything to ensure he has a great childhood. We both learned from our parents' mistakes, and, I for one, plan to be the best dad possible."

Part of doing that means, I need to make sure this baby's grandmother stays far, far away from my family.

Thirty-Three

Natasha ~ Present

"This is going to be cold," Dr. Richmond said, right before squirting goo onto my belly.

I sucked in my breath, because, *yes*, it was cold. I watched as she placed the end of the wand on my stomach and smeared the goo around, then turned my attention to the monitor, cognizant of Jericho's hand in mine and his face also turned toward the screen.

The room filled with a staticy sound, then, suddenly, there was a whooshing.

"That's your baby's heartbeat," the doctor informed us, and I felt my eyes fill with tears.

"Wow," Jericho whispered.

"That's *amazing*," I managed as the tears began to fall.

"Congratulations."

"Thank you," I said, bringing Jericho's hand to my cheek and turning toward him. "Can you believe it?"

Jericho's eyes were misty as well as he bent down to kiss me first on the forehead, then on the lips.

"We're going to be parents," he mused, and I nodded happily.

Never had I imagined when Jericho opened Prime Beef on Main Street, right across from Three Sisters, that we'd be here a year and a half later. I hadn't allowed myself to have this dream, not once I left him, and I was so grateful that he'd forgiven me, because now . . . I had everything I've ever wanted.

"I'll give you two a few minutes. Go ahead and get dressed, Natasha, and I'll meet you both in my office," Dr. Richmond said as she cleaned off my stomach with a tissue and rose from her stool.

"Thank you," I told her as I sat up and swung my legs over the side of the bed.

I waited until she left to stand up and take off the hospital gown, but before I could put my shirt back on, Jericho was kneeling before me, his hands on my waist. I grinned down at him when he placed a soft kiss on my belly, then felt that same tummy tingle when he looked up at me and took my left hand in his.

"Natasha Rose, ever since I bumped into you on purpose the first day of accounting class, I've been fascinated by you, and although we spent some time apart, I always held out hope that we'd end up back together. I missed you and now that I have you back, I never want to let you go. I can't wait to live our lives here, to raise our children, to grow old together. I feel like I was born to love you, and I want to show you that love every minute of every day. Marry me, and neither of us will ever be lonely again. I promise you a life full of love, laughter, and support."

I was full-on crying by the time he pulled a small velvet box out of his pocket and opened it to reveal a gorgeous, rose gold engagement ring with diamonds running along the band.

"Yes!" I cried then realized the sound was muffled by the hand covering my mouth. So, I lowered my right hand and extended the fingers on my left and said, "Yes," once more, louder this time.

I sniffled as he slid the ring on my finger, admired the shine for a moment, then jumped into his arms the moment he was back on his feet.

"I love you," I said, my hands coming up to pull his face down to mine for another, slightly wet kiss.

"I love you, too," Jericho replied between kisses. "Thanks for saying yes."

I laughed happily, then realized I still wasn't dressed and moved to get my clothes.

"When we tell this story, pretend I had clothes on," I said as I pulled my shirt over my head.

"You got it, babe," Jericho chuckled.

Once I was ready, we walked out of the room and down the hall to the doctor's office. I stood outside for a moment, unsure whether or not I should knock, but Dr. Richmond must have heard us because she called, "Come in."

Once we were settled, she looked at my hand, then up at the two of us with a friendly smile.

"Looks like congratulations are in order."

"Thank you," Jericho and I said, automatically reaching our hands out for each other.

"First things first, here are a few pictures I printed out of your baby. At coming appointments, we'll be able to use the 3D ultrasound machine to get better pictures, and usually, between your twelve or sixteen-week appointment, we'll be able to tell the gender of the baby, if that's something you'll want to know."

"Yes," I said, at the same time, Jericho exclaimed, "Absolutely!"

The doctor laughed and said, "Sounds good. We'll cross that bridge when we come to it. Until then, we'll plan to schedule once-a-month appointments for the first two trimesters, and here is a copy of *What to Expect When You're Expecting*, as well as some informational brochures for you both to start reading."

"Thank you so much," I said as Jericho reached over to gather everything off of the desk and placed it on his lap.

"Do you have any questions for me?" she asked.

"Um, yes, I didn't realize I was pregnant, and I've had some wine over the last few weeks, will that *harm* the baby in any way?" I asked nervously. This was a question that had been bothering me all day.

"No, small amounts of alcohol will not affect your baby's growth. I recommend that from this point forth you refrain from any heavy drinking, but a small glass of wine now and again won't hurt."

I nodded, and let out a relieved breath.

"Anything else?"

"Sex," Jericho spat out, as if he had to force himself to ask. "Will sex hurt the baby?"

Dr. Richmond smiled, and assured him, "Absolutely not. It's perfectly safe, and healthy, to have a normal sex life. In fact, once you're ready to give birth, it actually helps move things along."

Jericho looked pleased with this information.

"All right then, if there's nothing else, you can set up your next appointment at the front desk for one month from now. I suggest you take notes as you're reading and write down any questions that you have for me over the next few weeks, and bring them in with you for your next appointment."

"Sounds good, and thanks again, Dr. Richmond," Jericho said as he stood and shook her hand.

"Thank you," I mimicked, waving goodbye as I led us out of her office, eager to get to the car so I could start reading the material.

Thirty-Four

Jericho ~ Present

"I'm nervous," Natasha whispered, tugging on my hand to make me stop.

I turned and looked down at her with a reassuring smile.

"It's going to be okay, I've got you," I replied, trying to get her to start moving again, but she stayed rooted.

"He hates me," she said, her eyes wide and suspiciously misty.

Natasha had been pretty emotional over the last few days. Crying at television commercials, songs, and one time when she dropped her peanut butter sandwich on the floor. It was completely out of character for her, and I found it terribly endearing.

"Baby, he'll come around, I promise. Remember, it wasn't that long ago that Dru wanted to fry my heart up like bacon."

Natasha laughed at that. "She still kind of wants to."

"I know," I said with a chuckle, "which is why I go out of my way to be extra nice to her. Come on, Hector is a great guy, I swear it."

Natasha nodded and unstuck her feet, allowing me to lead her back into the kitchen at Prime Beef.

Hector was wearing his black chef coat, with Prime Beef stitched over his heart. He was talking to his sous chef and didn't see us until we were almost next to him. His head swung up, and he started to smile at me, then his gaze shifted so he saw Natasha and he shot me a frown.

"Hey," I said in greeting, my tone a warning for him to not be a dick.

"Jericho," he replied, his voice conveying his annoyance with me. "Ambush?"

"Let's go to the office for a minute," I suggested, aware of all the eyes in the kitchen on us.

"I'm pretty busy right now . . ."

"Hector, just give us a minute of your time, we'll be quick," I said, exasperated.

"Fine," Hector said grudgingly, holding out his hand to indicate we should go first.

Not trusting him to actually follow, I mimicked his gesture, smiling when he let out a frustrated breath, but started walking.

I looked down at Natasha, who was looking a little freaked, and gave her shoulder a reassuring squeeze before we followed him out and to my office.

"You've got your minute," Hector said, crossing his arms over his chest as he turned to face us.

"Quit being a dick," I managed, getting pissed off. "That's not who you are, and that's not who I want Natasha to think you are. We came here because you're one of the two most important people in my life, so not only do I want it to stay that way, but when something amazing happens, I want to be able to tell you about it. Since it's not only my news to share, I thought it was about time I brought the two of you together, and let Natasha be here to share our news as well."

Hector thawed a bit, but looked at Natasha and me suspiciously. "What news?"

"We're getting married," I said.

"And, having a baby," Natasha added, just like we'd talked about, but her voice wavered as she waited warily for Hector's reaction.

It took him a moment. He actually shook his head as if unsure he'd heard us correctly, then his gaze flew down to Natasha's left hand, before coming back up to look in my face.

"You're engaged *and* having a baby?" he asked, in total shock. Then, slowly, his lips turned up and his grin took up his entire face.

I heard Natasha breathe a sigh of relief, as my oldest friend came rushing forward to give me a crushing hug.

"Congratulations, *Papi*," he said with a laugh, and I hugged him back just as tightly.

"Thanks, brother."

Hector pulled back, still grinning like a lunatic, then let me go and turned to Natasha.

Before he could speak, she did.

"I don't blame you for not liking me. You're a good friend to Jericho, and as such, you were there for him when I left him and broke his heart. You shouldn't like me, at least, not for that . . . But, Jericho has said that in addition to being loyal, you're fair, and have a big heart. So, I'm hoping, eventually, you'll find it in your heart to give me a chance. I'm not going anywhere this time, I promise. I'm going to be Jericho's wife, and the mother of his children, and we both want you to be a part of that life. I understand it may take time, but I'll be here, if you're ever ready to get to know me now."

Hector looked shocked, and I had to pull her in for a quick hug and kiss before releasing her and waiting to see what he'd say.

Finally, he nodded.

"I appreciate your candor, and your understanding. It will take a little time for me, but, making this man happy is all I need from you to help move that along. He's always wanted to have a family, and you're giving him that, so thank you, *Natasha*, and congratulations."

"He already has a family in you. I hope you'll come to accept my sisters and I as well, and our growing family, because we're happy to have you."

With that said, seemingly unable to help herself, Natasha lurched forward and wrapped her arms around Hector's waist for a quick hug. Hector patted her awkwardly, then she released him and stepped back.

"Okay, our minute is up," I said, pleased with what had just transpired and hopeful that these two would eventually have at least an amicable relationship. "Now we're off to spread our good news around to Natasha's sisters and our friends. I'll see you before dinner service."

Hector nodded and said, "Congrats again, Jericho, you deserve all the happiness in the world."

Thirty-Five

Natasha ~ Present

Today had been a good day.

A great day.

The *best* day.

After finding out that *yes*, we are indeed pregnant, having Jericho propose, and having a somewhat scary, but positive, introduction to Hector, we'd gone to tell everyone else the news. Millie, Jackson, and Kayla were ecstatic, Dru a little less so, but still happy, and everyone at Three Sisters was thrilled at the prospect of another wedding, and a baby to be our mascot.

Mick was still in Philly, but we'd also told Rob, Jan, Ty, and Rebecca, although by video chat rather than in person. And, when Mick called to give Jericho an update, he'd shared the good news with him as well.

The only bleak spot on the day was that although he'd had a couple leads, Mick still hadn't been able to locate Jericho's mom.

Still, all in all, *best day ever.*

To top it off, we were laying on the couch, watching a singing competition, while I snacked on popcorn and Jericho rubbed my feet.

Pure bliss.

"You know, after today, I kind of hate myself for what I put us through," I told Jericho, not because I wanted him to argue, or say nice things about me, but because it was true.

I'd spent so long being afraid. Of being abandoned, of change, really, of allowing myself to really be happy. I'd been sabotaging my own happiness because of the lives my parents lived, rather than working to prove that I could do differently.

"I don't hate you," Jericho replied. "In fact, I love you more right this second than I ever have before."

"I feel the same," I assured him, then asked, "But doesn't it make you angry when you realize we could have been this happy the whole time?"

"No."

"Why not?" I asked, curious.

"Because being apart made it possible for us to be where we are today. We both accomplished great things professionally, and although we may not have been as fulfilled personally as we could've been, we found our support systems. Who knows how things would have played out? I, for one, couldn't be happier with where we are today."

"Me neither," I agreed softly.

Just then, Newt jumped up on the couch to see what we were doing. Ignoring the two of us, he went up on the back cushions and pawed his spot until it was to his liking, then laid down and closed his eyes.

Jericho found a tender place in my foot and rubbed it deeply, causing me to moan and slide a little farther down into the couch.

"Do you still want a dog?" he asked.

"Yeah, eventually."

"Big, small, or medium sized?"

"Hmmmm." I looked up as if deep in thought, then said, "Medium."

"Do you have a breed in mind?"

I shook my head.

"No, just a sweet dog that will be a good family dog. Mostly an indoor dog, who will sleep in bed with us."

"Oh yeah?"

"Of course, she's going to be part of the family."

"She? Okay. Noted."

"What does that mean?" I asked.

"Nothing, just that I'm listening and storing away information for future use," Jericho replied, then turned back to the TV. "What do you think of her?"

"I hope she wins it all," I said.

"I'm rooting for Victor to win."

I was about to argue when Jericho's phone rang.

"What's up, Renee?"

Renee was one of his hostesses at Prime Beef. After we'd shared our news, Jericho had gone into work while I did the same. At about eight thirty, he'd picked me up and brought me home, with takeout, so we could relax, eat dinner, and watch TV together.

When he disconnected, Jericho patted me on the foot, his face apologetic.

"Looks like I need to head back in," he said, and when I moved my feet off of him, he stood. "There's a guest at the restaurant who wants to talk to me. She wouldn't settle for the night manager, or Hector, so I'm going to go take care of it."

"Okay," I said, tilting my head back for the kiss he offered. "I'll probably finish this then go up and soak in the tub for a while."

"Sounds good, I'll be back as soon as I can. I'm sorry to have to leave."

"Hey, not feeling guilty for our jobs, remember. If anyone can understand the demands of the food service industry, it's me, right? Go do what you need to, Newt and I will be fine here," I assured him, gesturing to Newt, who didn't bother to open his eyes, let alone concur.

"Thanks, babe. Do you need anything?" When I shook my head, he said, "Well, if that changes, shoot me a text and I'll stop on the way home."

"Will do. I love you," I called as he headed toward the door.

"I love you, too."

Thirty-Six

Jericho ~ Past

"You go on outside now, while I take care of business," my mother said. Her eyes had that glassy look that I hated, and the tall guy with the big belly in our living room was giving me a look that said if I didn't get moving, he'd kick me until I did. So, I left.

It was already dark, and kinda cold. Although, if I had a jacket, it probably wouldn't be so bad.

"I hate her," I mumbled, then looked over my shoulder, sure I'd see her standing there, ready to smack the words out of my mouth.

My arms were skinny, but they were getting bigger. I'd started working out after school, after seeing how big some of the eighth graders at my school were. I'd followed some of the football players and found them all lifting weights and doing pushups and stuff, so I'd started hanging out and doing what they did.

At first, I'd thought they'd catch me and kick me out, I was only in sixth grade after all, and they usually didn't want nothing to do with us. But Bo, one of the biggest guys, lived in my same apartment building and said he'd *vouch* for me.

Whatever that meant.

I think it meant he knew who I was, knew who my mom was . . .

"It's better for him to come here and work out, gain some muscle so he can take care of himself, then end up on the streets with the druggies, or worse," I'd heard Bo tell the coach one day.

Anyway, because of that, no one gave me any problems. I'd been going there every day after school, and although the only difference so far was that my body was always sore, I felt like change was coming.

But now, school was closed and my mom wanted me gone, so I had no choice.

My stomach growled, and I tried to remember the last time I'd eaten. It had been a couple days at least. The school offered free lunches for people in need, but my mom didn't fill out the forms cause, *"We don't need no charity from no damn do-gooders,"* so I usually only ate if she remembered to go grocery shopping, or bring something home.

I was thinking I needed to get a job. That way, I could buy food for myself and eat it when she wasn't around.

"Hey, kid, come here," a man yelled, but I just started walking faster and turned the corner, then I started running.

"You cold, baby?" one of the women on the corner asked, but I ignored her, too.

Some of these people were nice and tried to help, but I'd met too many of the other kind. The ones who wanted me to sell drugs at school, or suck dick for five bucks, so I'd stopped talking to anyone on these streets.

I'd run about four blocks when I needed to stop and catch my breath. I looked around, trying to figure out where I was. When I recognized the deli, I let out a sigh of relief. This street wasn't so bad.

I kept walking, making a game out of kicking trash on the sidewalk, when a sound had me looking up and to the left.

A boy about my size was waving at me from behind a dumpster.

At first, I thought about running in the other direction, 'cause who knew who, or what, was in the alley with that kid, then I heard him ask, "You're Jericho, right?"

I paused, trying to decide what the smart thing to do was, then shrugged and walked closer to the boy.

"Who're you?" I asked, looking past him into the alley, relieved when I didn't see anyone else.

"I'm Hector," he said, "I'm in your math class."

I squinted, trying to make him out better in the dark.

"Oh yeah, you sit next to Gunther."

Hector was pretty new to the school, and was just as quiet as I was, so we'd never really met before.

"Yeah," he replied with a shrug. "What are you doing out here?"

I mimicked his movement and said, "Just needed to get out of the house for a while. You?"

"Same."

Just then, my stomach growled again, and I flushed with embarrassment.

"The guy at the deli usually leaves the food he's gonna throw out just inside the back door, for me and some of the other kids around here. If we don't eat it, he throws it away, then puts more out the next day. He won't care if you eat some."

Hector started walking through the alley, to where I assumed the back door of the deli was, but I stood still watching him, suddenly worried that I'd been wrong to trust him, and it was a trap.

After all, why would a man give food to kids, without wanting something in return.

I watched Hector open the door and disappear for a second, then come back out with a hand full of bread and meat. He walked toward me, holding it out, but I kept my gaze trained on the door.

"It's legit," he promised once he was back in front of me. To prove it, Hector put some of the meat in his mouth, chewed and swallowed, then grinned. "See."

Too hungry to stop, I took the food from his hands and began to eat it as fast as I could.

"Easy," Hector said. "You'll get sick if you eat too fast. That's what happened to me."

"You live around here?" I asked between bites.

"Yeah, in *the bricks*," he said, referring to another apartment complex a couple blocks from mine. "You?"

"Commons," I replied.

Hector nodded, indicating he knew where that was, then asked, "You want to head down to the park and hang out for a while?"

"Sure," I said, happy to have a full belly and a new friend.

Little did I know, when I returned home that night, I'd find out that my mom had been arrested and would serve her first stint in jail for soliciting a police officer.

Thirty-Seven

Natasha ~ Present

I'd finished my bath and was lying in bed reading *What to Expect When You're Expecting,* when I heard a commotion downstairs. Thinking Jericho was back, I placed the book on the nightstand and got out of bed, making my way down the stairs.

The light in the kitchen that I left on for him was still on, but he wasn't in there, so I crossed to the living room, about to call out his name, when a movement by the windows caused me to turn that way.

I froze at the sight of a woman, a very skinny woman with frail hair and an angry expression on her face.

"Who are you?" I asked, my mind racing as it searched for a memory of the nearest weapon.

"Who the fuck is you?" she countered, her voice deep and raspy, like someone who'd been smoking for decades.

I reached for my phone in my pocket, then realized that I was wearing my nightgown and did not have pockets, *or* my phone.

"You're trespassing. You need to leave this house," I said, trying to keep my tone firm. Unyielding.

She wasn't impressed.

"No, you need to go get my boy and bring him here to me. Tell him his momma's come, just as she promised."

My eyes widened in horror when I realized that *this* was Jericho's mother. How such a tall, gorgeous, wonderful man like my fiancé came from *this* woman, baffled me.

"Ah, I can see you got your judgy pants on, huh, Ms. Oklahoma or some shit . . . Don't go looking down your nose at me. You just go on and bring my boy to me."

"He's not here," I said, then snapped my mouth shut.

Shit. I probably shouldn't have said that, I could have said I was going to get him and went and got my phone.

"I mean, let me go see if I can find him," I amended, and started to back out of the room.

"Oh, *no*, Oklahoma, you go ahead and sit your pretty face down there and we'll wait for Ric to get here."

"I could go call him," I offered, trying one last thing as I sat on the nearest chair.

"Nah, I think I'll go for the . . . element of surprise," she said, coming close enough so I could see her face.

It was a face with many, many years on it. Hard years. It was weathered and rough and I wondered what life had been like for her in prison.

"So, Oklahoma, you Jericho's piece like full time, or does he have a bunch like you coming and going?"

I wasn't sure what I should say, or how honest I could be. I knew Jericho didn't want anything to do with her, so I couldn't imagine he'd want her knowing information about his life. Still, maybe if she knew I was going to be her daughter-in-law, it would change her behavior toward me.

"Actually, I'm his fiancée, we're getting married," I said, hopeful that she would show the tiniest bit of motherly happiness.

Instead, she hurried over to me and picked up my hand, her eyes widening with glee at the ring on my finger.

I snatched my hand back and sat on it.

"Mmmmm, I see you, girl. Got yourself a good thing goin' here . . . leading my son around by his dick, getting fancy rings and big-ass houses. We're just alike, you and I."

I cringed at her words, and she smiled hatefully.

"Don't like that, do ya, but it's true all the same. Don't see you tied to some dock worker living in a trailer park, do I? Nope, Ms. Oklahoma is bringing my boy to heel and keeping money that is rightfully mine away from *me*. Is that why he said no? You in his ear, Oklahoma?"

"No, I have nothing to do with your relationship with your son. That's between you and Jericho."

Before she could reply, her phone rang. She glared at me, then flipped it open and said, "What?"

Her face got angrier as she listened, then she hung up and swore a string of words that would've made a sailor proud.

She flipped the phone shut again without another word.

"Looks like Ric's goon is making problems for me. That was my parole officer. He needs to see me."

Relieved that she had to leave, I tried to look contrite as I said, "I'll tell Jericho you're looking for him as soon as he gets home."

"That's cute, Oklahoma, you're as dumb as you look. Uh-uh, missy, you're coming with me as insurance."

"No!" I cried, standing and placing my hand on my stomach reflexively.

Jericho's mom tracked my movement, and if was possible, her

smile became even more horrible.

"Ah, *bun in the oven*, that's why Jericho's allowing himself to get saddled with a piece like you. Even better," she said, stepping toward me. I took a step away. "Double the insurance."

"I'm not going anywhere with you," I argued.

Then I watched in horror as she pulled a small handgun out of the back of her jeans and pointed it at me.

Right at my stomach.

"Oh, I think you are," she said, then flicked her wrist toward the door. "Move."

Thirty-Eight

Jericho ~ Present

By the time he'd arrived at Prime Beef, the customer had left.

"That's so weird," Renee said. "She was standing right there when I called, so she knew you were on the way."

"Okay, I'm going to go back to my office for a few minutes, just in case she's in the bathroom or something. Let me know if she shows back up."

I'd spent a good thirty minutes in my office, then checking reports in the POS. Once we were closed for the night, and it was obvious the lady was gone, I said goodbye to Renee and headed back home.

I figured Natasha had fallen asleep by now, but was thinking of all the fun ways I could wake her up when I pulled up to the house and noticed the lights were on and the front door was wide open.

Fear had my heart pounding in my ears as I jumped out of the still running car and ran for the house.

"Natasha!" I began yelling her name over and over as soon as my feet hit the steps.

I ran inside, looking around, but not seeing anything out of order, so I kept going up the stairs to the bedroom.

The covers on the bed were flipped over, like Natasha had been inside and but had gotten out for one reason or another. The table lamp was on and her book was on the table. I crossed to the bathroom, and although the scent of her bath bomb still filled the air, the lights were off and the room was empty.

I went back into the room and walked closer to the bed, that's when I noticed her phone on the table behind her book. I picked it up and looked at it, but the most recent call had been when I'd called earlier to see if she was ready to be picked up.

I kept calling her name as I ran back down the stairs.

Her purse was on the counter where she'd put it when we'd gotten home.

Her shoes were by the door.

I ran back outside, jumping off the porch rather than bothering with the stairs, and started running around the back of the house.

I checked the back porch, the backyard, side of the house, even started running farther out on the property, even though I knew there was no reason for her to be back there. Although, there was no logical explanation for what was happening either.

Going on autopilot, I pulled my phone out of my pocket and pushed Hector's number.

"Hey, Jericho, sorry I missed you earlier, I had a dessert emergency," Hector said as way of greeting, but I cut him off.

"She's gone," I managed, my tone full of the desperation and panic that I was feeling.

"What do you mean, *gone?*" Hector asked, his voice filled with anger, and I knew what he was thinking.

"No, not like that," I said, standing back in front of my house, my gaze searching the dark perimeter. "Like, *missing*. The bed was half made, her phone is on the dresser, her purse in the kitchen. When I got home, the front door was wide open. *Hector . . .*" I choked his name as fire burned in my throat.

"Just stay put, I'm on my way," Hector ordered, his voice commanding and firm.

It helped some of the panic subside, and I said, "I'm going to hang up and call Mick."

"Don't leave until I get there. Five minutes."

I nodded my affirmation, then hung up and dialed Mick.

"Smythe," Mick said grumpily, and I could tell I woke him up.

"Sorry to wake you, but Natasha is gone. Missing. Have you found my mother?" I asked, but heard a beep in my ear and looked at the phone to see it was Hector.

I clicked over.

"I talked to Renee," he said when he heard me answer. "I asked her to describe the woman, and I hate to say it, Jericho, but it sounds like your mother was the one who had you called out to the restaurant."

"Then came to my house after I said I was on my way? Why?" I asked as I paced my driveway.

"So she could ambush you at your place, catch you off-guard? I don't know."

"Shit, I'm on the other line with Mick, let me tell him."

"Okay, I'm two minutes out."

"Mick," I called as I clicked over. "It sounds like my mom was here and I'm guessing either her, or one of her associates, has Natasha."

"I talked to her parole officer this evening and he said he has a meeting with her tomorrow, so if she was there, and had Natasha, at least we know where she'll be at ten tomorrow."

"I'm getting in the car now."

"No," Mick said sharply.

"What? What do you mean no? I'm coming to Philly, Mick."

"Dammit, Jericho, you hired me to do a job, so let me do it. If your unstable mother who's after money has Natasha, she's probably planning to hit you up for ransom. Rather than riding up here guns blazing, how about you let me get with her parole officer and get this all sorted out. If she catches sight of you in town, she may do something more dangerous than she already has. Let us handle it."

"*Fuck!*" I yelled, as Hector's truck pulled up and he jumped out much like I had.

"What?" Hector asked as he ran to my side.

"Mick says they're headed that way, but he wants me to stay put."

Hector took my phone out of my hand and put it to his ear. "Mick," he said, then listened. "Yeah, I'll be with him. No, we won't head that way, but we can't keep this from her sisters, that wouldn't be right. Yeah, I understand that, but if I were in their shoes, I'd want to know. Be careful, that woman shouldn't be underestimated. Yeah, here you go."

He handed the phone back to me.

"Yeah," I said to Mick.

"I'll bring her home, Jericho, yeah?" Mick said, his voice full of conviction. "Tell Dru, too."

"Yeah, okay," I replied, feeling utterly helpless.

"I'll call you first thing," he assured me, then hung up.

"Come on, let's get you inside and get some coffee on. It's gonna be a long night," Hector said, and I followed him as I searched Jackson's number.

Thirty-Nine

Natasha ~ Present

We'd been driving for a few hours, me sitting as far away from Jericho's mother as possible on the bench seat. I was practically hugging the door. I'd thought about trying to jump out and make a run for it, but didn't want to chance hurting the baby.

I was tired, and kept forcing myself awake each time I started nodding off.

"I need to go to the bathroom," I said, thinking we could pull over at the next gas station and I could tell the person working there I was being held against my will.

The more the idea took share, the more hopeful I became.

"No," she stated, her eyes on the road, an unlit cigarette dangling out of her mouth.

We'd gotten into it when we'd started out and she'd tried to light up in the car. I didn't think she'd listen to my pleas about no smoking for the baby's health, but she'd rolled her eyes and left it unlit.

"Please," I asked. "You've been pregnant, so you know how much you need to use the bathroom. It's been hours and I've been holding it for the last thirty miles."

"You think I'm dumb or something, Oklahoma?" She sneered. "First off, that baby ain't no bigger than a pea right now, so no way it's sitting on your bladder or nothing like if you were further along. Second, you're thinking of calling for help the second I stop, and then I lose my chance to trade you to Jericho for the money I need."

"I don't know why you keep insisting on calling me Oklahoma. I'm not from, nor have I ever been to Oklahoma. I've also never been in a pageant, so you're wrong about that, too. My name is Natasha, I'm engaged to your son and carrying his baby, and he's not going to be too happy with you for doing all of this. Now, the least you can do after *kidnapping me from my own home*, is let me go to the bathroom."

I was tired, hungry and beyond irritated, and dammit, I really did have to pee.

"Guess you got a little sass after all. That's good. Ric needs a little sass, else he'd be walking all over you, like men do. Still, I'm calling bullshit . . . So, if you really have to go, I'll pull over right here and you can go on the side of the road. Then, I can grab a smoke and we'll be on our way."

"You want me to pee on the side of the road? There's no coverage," I argued.

"It's dark, no one will see anything."

"Fine," I said, deflated that my plan hadn't worked. It looked like I needed to wait until we were in the city to try and find someone to help me.

She pulled over and we both hopped out. She waved the gun at me, as if to warn me not to run, then lit her cigarette.

I scowled and tried to find the place where I'd be most hidden from people passing by and lifted my nightgown.

"Don't get any on your feet now," Jericho's mom called with a cackle.

God, I hate her.

Once my bladder was relieved, I walked back to the car and got into the passenger side, not wanting to be around her *or* her smoke.

I wondered what Jericho was doing. *Did he come home yet and find the house empty? Does he think I left him again without so much as a word?*

I worried my bottom lip as I thought about how upset he would be.

Plus, with Mick in Philly looking for his mom, he'd never expect her to have been the one who took me from our house. I hated to think what he must be going through.

"Let's get this show on the road," Jericho's mom said as she slammed her way into the car.

Unable to stand being in her presence another second, I crawled over the seat and got into the back, laying across the long seat and closing my eyes.

"C'mon, Ms. Oklahoma, time to get up."

That scratchy voice pulled me from seat and I sat up, blinking my eyes open, then shut when the sunlight stung them. I waited a few seconds, then opened them slowly, to give them time to adjust.

We were parked on the street, alongside a dilapidated old apartment building, and it was early enough that the only people on the streets were the ones who were just now coming home, either from work or partying.

And although I wanted to scream for help, it looked like the kind of place where screams wouldn't garner much attention.

"C'mon, you're gonna walk in front of me, and I'll tell you where to go. And, I gotta say, Oklahoma, even if someone sees the gun, they aren't gonna do shit, so don't go getting any wild ideas.

The last thing you want to do is be running around these streets in nothing but your nightie, without me there to protect ya."

Looking around, I believed her, so I walked and went where she told me to.

"Up the stairs . . . down the hall . . . to the left . . . that one, number twelve."

She knocked on the door with the tip of her gun, then we waited. A few seconds later, there was a crash, bang, and a round of swearing. Then, the door opened to reveal an older man, with a gray beard, tired eyes, and a scowling face. He was wearing well-worn jeans that had been pulled on, but not fastened.

"The fuck you doin' here?" he asked Jericho's mom.

"Need to stash somethin' here for a little while so I can go see my parole officer."

"What?" he asked, scratching his butt.

"Her," she replied, and I squeaked.

What the hell? She's going to leave me here with some strange old biker dude?

"No, that's okay," I said. "I'll just come with you."

As much as I hated her, I felt better with the devil I knew, than the devil I didn't.

She scoffed.

"Yeah, like I can show up with you. You'd go blabbing that I left town *and* took you against your will for money." She turned her attention to the man and promised, "My son will give us the money we need in exchange for the beauty queen here. Alls I gotta do is go smooth things over with my PO, show him I'm here and doin' fine, and then we can get this settled and get the fuck outta dodge. I just need you to watch her for a little while. Hour, tops."

Biker dude looked at her, then at me, his gaze going down to my bare feet, then up my legs, over my nightgown, until it settled on my face.

He nodded, and I shuddered.

Forty

Jericho ~ Present

I sat up and looked around, momentarily disoriented as I took in what was happening around me.

My living room was full of people.

Jackson and Kayla were on an air mattress, still asleep, and Dru was sleeping in the chair next to the couch, her head tilted in what looked like an uncomfortable position. Newt was in her lap, staring back at me with his green eyes.

I shifted into sitting and looked into the kitchen, where Hector and Millie stood, working together on what I assumed was breakfast.

I picked my phone up off the table, hoping for a text or missed call, but there was nothing. With a sigh, I stood and stretched quietly, so as not to wake anyone else. We'd been up pretty late last night, everyone having rushed over after I called Jackson to let him know what was happening.

Needing fuel, I headed into the kitchen.

"Hey," I greeted, crossing to kiss Millie lightly on the head. "Did you get any sleep?"

She shook her head and gave a small smile.

"I baked a lot."

"You should go lay down, try and get some rest."

"I can't," Millie said, her eyes full of worry, and I hugged her briefly before giving a slight nod.

"What about you? How long have you been up?" I asked Hector as I filled my coffee cup.

"A little while," Hector replied. "We thought we'd make everyone breakfast."

Before I could turn, Millie stopped me and held my cup, then she sprinkled something in it and said, "Here."

"What's that?"

"Cinnamon."

"In my coffee?" I asked, about to toss it and get another cup.

"Just a touch," Millie replied. "It's a little sweet, and a little spice, to bring the flavor up a notch. It's good for you, just try it."

"Uh, thanks," I said, then left them to do their thing and went out onto the patio.

Once outside, I sat down on the chair and took a tentative sip.

"Huh, that's actually pretty good," I murmured.

I wondered where Natasha was and what she was going through, and wished she were there beside me.

I heard the door open and turned to see Dru coming through it, a blanket wrapped around her shoulders and coffee mug in her hands. She crossed in front of me and sat on the loveseat, moving her head from side to side as if her neck were bothering her.

"Morning," I said.

"Morning," she replied softly, looking out over the railing as she took a sip. "Hear anything?"

I sighed.

"No, not yet."

Dru nodded and said, "She'll be okay."

"Yeah," I agreed softly. "My mom's a junkie and overall disappointment, but I can't see her harming Natasha. She wants money, and thinks this is her best shot at getting it. I just hate the thought of her being out there, alone with my mother, doing God knows what."

I felt the back of my eyes burn and struggled for control.

Dru's hand hit my back and began rubbing it in small, circular motions.

"She doesn't have anything. Her purse, her jacket . . . shoes," On that last word, I choked and took in a deep breath.

"You know, when our dad left, Natasha was young. Too young to fully understand what was happening. Millie was devastated. She'd been Daddy's girl, and they'd done everything together. And when he left like that, Millie sat outside on the stoop, all night, waiting for him to come back. She was crushed when he didn't. At first, she blamed our mom, and eventually, she became numb, pretended he'd never even existed. Me, on the other hand, from the second he left, I blocked it all out. All emotion, all thoughts of him, all the memories. I went on as if nothing happened. I guess my way of coping, was not coping at all . . ." Dru paused, causing me to look at her profile, then she shook her head and continued, "But, Natasha? Natasha got mad. She saw what his leaving did to Millie, to Mom, and I guess in a way, to me, and she *hated* him. She was the one to help us all adjust. She'd crawl into bed with Mom when she was sad, help distract Millie in the kitchen when she needed it, and she allowed me to live in my fantasy land where life was still perfect and we were all happy. Natasha's always been the strongest of all of us. *She's going to be okay,*" she said again, this time with conviction.

I reached out and took her hand in mine, and we sat there, drinking our coffee, giving each other support.

After about ten minutes, Millie popped her head out and said, "Breakfast is ready."

"Okay," I said, shooting Dru a grateful smile as I released her hand and stood. "Thanks, Dru."

"Anytime, that's what family is for," she replied, then went through the door as I held it open for her.

Once we were back inside, I realized everyone was now awake and my house was a bustle of movement. Everyone was helping take the food, dishes, silverware, and drinks to the dining room table, and then we all found a place and sat.

Unsure of what to do, but feeling like I should say something, I looked around the table at Natasha's family, and my best friends, and said, "I can't tell you how much it means to me that you all came the second you heard about Natasha. We're going to get her back, and I know together, we'll do whatever it takes to make sure she's okay. I'm thankful for all of you, and for this meal that Hector and Millie made to give us all the strength we need to get through the day. So . . . let's eat."

It wasn't quite a prayer, but since the only praying I'd ever done was when I begged God to help me make it through another day as I child, I thought it was pretty good.

We began passing dishes of eggs, potatoes, breakfast meats, pancakes, and really, more food than an army of men could have eaten, and dug in. Mostly, we listened as Kayla chattered about the dreams she'd had the night before, but it was a nice distraction, all the same.

My phone rang and I stood, pulling it from my pocket to look at the screen.

"It's Mick."

Forty-One

Natasha ~ Present

"I'll be back," Jericho's mom said, laying a long, wet, quite disgusting kiss on her biker before walking out the door and leaving me behind.

I stood there, at the entrance to his apartment, unsure of what to do next. Afraid to move and call attention to myself, and wondering if he'd notice if I slipped out the door.

"What's your name?" the man asked gently, causing me to look up.

He was standing before me, with a shirt on now, running his hand through his beard as he watched me warily.

"Natasha," I replied, still stuck in place.

"Come on in, Natasha, it's not the Ritz, but you should be able to find a clean place to sit."

"Maybe I should go?" I asked, not ready to trust him.

"I wouldn't, not in this neighborhood. Have a seat, I'll be right back."

I walked in, looking around the small apartment and seeing that it was indeed neat. There were no beer bottles stacked up, or drug paraphernalia on the coffee table, which, if I was honest, was what I was half expecting to see.

Instead, there were pictures of what looked like grandchildren on his TV, and a couple Harley Davidson magazines on the table.

I sat down on the couch and numbly watched the news playing on the television.

"Here," he said, coming back in and throwing a pair of pajama pants in my lap, as well as a robe. "Those are my daughter's, so they should fit." He added a pair of socks and I almost whimpered with gratitude. I hadn't realized how cold my feet were until I saw those socks.

I put them on first, ignoring the black dirt on the bottom of my feet, then pulled the pants on under my nightgown.

He'd left again, but came back once I was dressed, a bottle of water in his hand.

"I'm Gregory," the man said. "Drink this, I'm sure you need it."

I broke the seal on the water, then took a tentative sip, before taking a few gulps.

"Easy," Gregory said, and I noticed he had a phone to his ear and a business card in his hand. "Yeah, this is Gregory. The girl, *Natasha,* is here . . . No, she went to see her PO. She won't be gone long, so you best hurry."

I watched him, initially thinking that he was selling me off to someone else, ready to bolt out of this seat and knock him down if necessary, then he looked at me, and I swear, I could see kindness there.

He was nothing like Jericho's mother.

"That was your PI friend, Mick, darlin'. He came by yesterday, then called last night and told me to call him if I happened to catch sight of you. He's on his way."

I started to tremble, a little at first, then in big, rocking waves. I sat there for what felt like forever, holding my water bottle and looking at, but not watching, the news, until finally there was a knock on the door.

I stood up, then sat back down, thinking, *oh God, what if it's her and not Mick,* then Gregory opened the door and Mick stepped in.

He was a formidable-looking man. Large in size and stature, with muscles that didn't quit, dark hair, and a gruff voice. If you met him in a dark alley, you'd run in the other direction, but his face was kind, and his light-green eyes mesmerizing, and in that moment, he was the best thing I'd ever seen.

I didn't know him well, in fact, we'd only ever said a few words to each other, but I leapt up and ran to him, not pausing before I rushed into his arms and held on for dear life.

"There's a lass," Mick said, more softly than I knew he could speak, as he patted my back reassuringly. "Thanks, Gregory. I talked to the PO, so she shouldn't be darkening your door again today. I'm going to get this one outta here."

I felt Mick lead me out of the apartment, and turned quickly to say, *"Thank you,"* to Gregory, before I let Mick take me down the stairs and out of the apartment complex to where his truck was waiting.

He helped me inside, then rounded the truck and got in the driver's seat. When we were off the streets and turning onto the highway, he handed me his phone and said, "You should give Jericho a call."

"Thanks," I said, thinking I could say that to him every hour of every day and it still wouldn't be enough.

"It's Mick," I heard Jericho say, before he put the phone to his ear and said, "Hello."

"Jericho," I managed, my voice breaking.

"Tash," he replied, his cracking with emotion as well. "He's got you?"

"Yeah," I said, then I started crying so hard I could no longer make sounds that formed words.

"Tasha, baby, you're okay," Jericho said soothingly, and I wanted to see him, to touch him so badly, that I started crying harder.

Knowing I wasn't going to stop anytime soon, I thrust the phone toward Mick.

"It's me," Mick said. "She's good. Unharmed, but shook up. No, she wasn't there, dropped Natasha with the guy she's currently shacked up with and went to see her PO, who was waiting to take her back into custody. Yeah, we're headed straight for ya, no stops unless she needs to. Yup. Later."

"Your family's at Jericho's so we'll go straight there," Mick said, his tone soothing as he spoke to me. "You can lay down if you need to, just holler if you need to stop for anything: food, drink, facilities . . . whatever."

I laid down, careful not to take up too much of his space in the cab of the truck, and when his hand patted my shoulder, offering me comfort, I took it, then I dozed off.

Forty-Two

Jericho ~ Present

*I*t turned out that it hadn't been Mick calling, it was Natasha, using his phone. She was with him and she was safe.

I'd hung up and told everyone what was going on, which caused shouts of happiness and an overall sense of relief to fall over the house. Dru and Millie had embraced, shedding a few tears over the knowledge that their sister was on her way home.

And I'd started cleaning.

My hands were shaking and I felt anxious, and since I needed to do something to keep myself busy until Mick and Natasha arrived, I started in the kitchen and worked my way upstairs.

I was in the closet, hanging the last of Natasha's things and putting her suitcases in the attic, when Jackson called up the stairs, "They're here."

I ran down the stairs, skipping steps as I went, until jumping over the last few and onto the landing. Everyone was already standing at the door, but they parted when they saw me, allowing me to make my way to the front.

Mick had just gotten out of the truck and was walking around the hood, when Natasha's door opened and she stepped down.

She had on her nightgown, with an oversized robe and too-long pajama pants on, along with some socks. She looked, tired, frazzled, and utterly beautiful.

I was there before she could take another step, pulling her into my arms and hugging her tightly.

"Are you okay? I love you. Did she hurt you? I'll kill her. I love you."

Natasha laughed as I babbled, and I swung her up into my arms, not wanting her to walk in just socks, and carried her to the house where everyone was practically busting at the seams to see her and touch her for themselves.

Once we crossed the threshold I put her down, and she was swept into hugs and kisses.

I could see she was feeling overwhelmed.

"Okay, guys, I know we're all happy she's home, but let's get her inside and comfortable," I said, then took her hand and kissed her knuckles. "What do you need?"

"A shower, and a fire to burn these clothes," Natasha replied.

"Done," I said, then, knowing everyone was still a little on edge and needed something to keep busy, I ordered, "Millie and Hector, you're on lunch. Dru, Kayla, can you go upstairs and get the shower heating up? Jackson, start the fire out back in the pit. And, Mick, what do you need? Gold, the shirt off my back, tequila? Say it and it's yours."

"I could use a beer."

"In the fridge," I said, then walked up the stairs, still holding Natasha's hand. Once we got in the room, Natasha walked into the bathroom and said, "Thanks," stopping to kiss Kayla and Dru on their cheeks.

"Anything else?" Dru asked as they left Natasha alone.

"I guess just see if Millie and Hector need anything. Thanks," I said, then followed Natasha into the bathroom.

"You need anything else?" I asked gently as she stepped under the steaming spray.

"No, I'll be down in a minute," she said with a small smile.

"I'll just take these then," I said, picking up the clothes. "Holler if you need anything."

I went downstairs and outside to where Mick and Jackson were standing by the fire pit. Without missing a beat, I crossed the patio and threw the clothes into the flame.

Mick handed me a beer, which I accepted, and the three of us stood there, sipping beer, watching the cotton material turn to ash. Once there was nothing left, we turned to join the others inside.

True to her word, Natasha was back with us in no time at all, fresh and clean with her hair pulled back in a small ponytail.

"Better?" I asked, meeting her in the middle of the living room.

"So much," she replied with a smile as she tilted her head back to look at me. "I love you."

"I love you, too, Natasha, more than I can ever express in words . . . When I got home and realized you were missing, it was like my heart had been stolen from my chest."

"I know," Natasha said softly, "I felt the same way. And all I kept thinking about, was how much time we've lost . . . I don't want to lose anymore."

"We won't," I promised.

"Marry me," she said, her fingers coming up to trace my face, as if committing it to memory.

"I think we already had this conversation," I said, smiling for the first time in twenty-four hours.

"I mean now, right away. I don't want to wait any longer."

"I'll see what I have to do to get the license and find a Justice of the Peace," I replied, willing to marry her whenever and however she wanted. The sooner the better.

"You don't have to do that," Millie said, her arm around Jackson's waist as they watched us. "We know of a place you can get married in two short weeks."

Jackson nodded.

"We aren't going to take your wedding, Mills," Natasha said with a laugh. "But thank you, that's very sweet."

"You don't have to take it, but you can share it," Millie informed us.

Natasha put her arms around me and snuggled in, looking at her family as she said, "Thank you all so much for being here, not just for me, but for Jericho, and for showing him what having a true family is all about. This is what I've been trying to get him to understand, although I never thought I'd have to get kidnapped to prove it."

Everyone chuckled.

I lowered my head to cover her lips with mine, starting off slow and soft, then deepening the kiss, putting everything I'd felt over the last twenty-four hours into it.

"I love you so much. Thank you for giving me your family, and for giving me *you* back. You're the touch of cinnamon, that extra bit of flavor I need to spice up my life. *You're* good for me."

Natasha

After my crash course in why Jericho's mother is never going to be grandma material, I went back to see Dr. Richmond, to make sure the baby was safe and there were no stress-related issues.

The baby was fine and everything was still on track.

Jericho and I had agreed that we did not want to takeover Millie and Jackson's wedding. Although the gesture was sweet, they'd put a lot of thought and effort into planning their perfect day, and it would be just that, perfect . . . *for them.*

Instead, Jericho and I *had* gone to the Justice of the Peace, with Millie, Dru, Jackson, Kayla, and Hector in attendance. Jackson and Hector had been Jericho's witnesses, while Millie and Dru had been mine.

Afterwards, we had a small dinner party at Prime Beef that included our family and friends as well as the staff of Three Sisters and Prime Beef. It had been lovely and perfect. Exactly what we both wanted.

Now, we were married, living in our dream home and having

a baby.

No waiting required. We were ready to get to the part where we *lived* our lives.

Now, I stood at the altar next to Dru, wearing our pretty mint-green dresses, *which matched Mick's eyes*, and waited for our eldest sister to walk down the aisle to marry the man of her dreams.

When I heard *The Wedding March* begin to play, I leaned forward so I could see Jackson's face when he saw Millie in her dress for the first time.

He didn't disappoint.

His face turned dreamy and he began to tear up as she and Kayla walked toward him down the aisle.

I turned to look at my sister, who was positively glowing as she marched toward her happily ever after, then turned my attention to my husband. The tall, gorgeous, dark man in the front row, who was watching me with an expression full of love and adoration.

"If I wasn't so happy for you all, I'd be sick to my stomach," Dru whispered in my ear.

"Shhh," I hissed. "You can't say that right when Millie's about to get married."

I looked at her and realized she was either about to bust out laughing or burst into tears.

"Pull it together, Drusilla," I warned, then turned my attention back to the ceremony and hoped we'd make it through without any embarrassing moments.

We did, and it was a beautiful ceremony, held in the church that Kayla had been baptized in, with all of Jackson's family in attendance.

For the reception, they'd decided on an outdoor venue, and Three Sisters Catering, along with Party with Laurel, a company run by a woman Dru knew, had turned the space into a magical wonderland.

We'd put up tents, just in case, with pretty white lights hanging throughout. There was a stage for the band, as well as a dance floor, and tables strewn about for the full-service dinner we'd be serving.

Decorated with mint green and pink, it was romantic in a way that fit Jackson and Millie perfectly.

When an Elvis impersonator got on stage and started singing *Love Me Tender*, I thought Millie might faint, but she made it through her first dance as Jackson's wife with a beaming smile on her face.

We laughed when Dru caught the bouquet and started blowing kisses to the crowd, then at Mick's scowl when he stood at the edge of the group of men vying for the boutonniere and Jackson turned and threw it right at him.

As Jericho spun me around the dance floor, I reveled at how far my sisters and I had come since our mother had passed away. How much our lives had changed. How much she missed. And, although it made me sad, I knew she was smiling down on us, happy that we were finding our own happiness.

"Hey," Jericho whispered, his mouth close enough to my ear to give me tingles. "Three o'clock."

"What? It's like nine o'clock at night, what are you talking about?"

Jericho sighed.

"No, *look*, at my three o'clock."

"I don't know what you're talking about."

Jericho have me a look of exasperation, then moved us around and jerked his head to the right. I turned my face to see what he was talking about, and watched as Hector took my sister's hand and led Dru onto the dance floor.

My mouth may have dropped open, and I maneuvered Jericho so I could see what happened next.

They stopped at the middle of the floor and Hector put Dru's hand on his shoulder, then his on her waist, and clasped her other hand. Then they began to move.

"Wow," I breathed. "Hector has some moves."

"Yeah, we took classes at the Y when we were fifteen. That's where all the girls went after school, so that's where we went."

"Are you saying *you* have moves like *that*?" I asked, my eyes still on the couple gliding around the floor.

"Hells yeah, baby," Jericho said, then moved one of my hands to his shoulder and took the other in his and off we went.

I laughed happily as we danced, matching Hector and Dru as we followed them around the floor.

"You're just full of surprises, aren't you, Mr. Smythe?"

"That's not all I have in store, Mrs. Smythe."

"Really? What other surprise do you have for me?" I asked, ready to try anything with him.

"I talked to Dr. Richmond, and she gave the all clear for you to travel."

"Where am I traveling to?" I asked, enjoying our banter.

"You didn't get the big wedding or fancy reception, but I'll be damned if my wife's not going to get her honeymoon."

I stopped dancing.

"Honeymoon?" I asked, unable to hide my excitement.

"Yes, ma'am, tomorrow morning, we are leaving for a two-week vacation to . . . Bali," Jericho said, pausing for effect. Then resumed dancing.

"Bali, *oh my God*, that's amazing."

"Yup, monkeys, elephants, and me."

"Well, they're all kind of the same thing," I joked, then threw myself into his arms. "Thank you, seriously. I cannot wait to go to Bali with you."

"My beautiful bride, the world is yours for the taking, and I plan to give it to you."

Stay tuned for Dru's story, A Splash of Vanilla, coming in 2018!

Check out the first chapter for Bethany Lopez's, *More than Exist.*

More Than Exist

PROLOGUE

What do you do when your perfect life is shattered in an instant?

A year ago, I got the knock at the door that every person fears. It was a rainy Sunday morning and I was lounging around, still in pajamas, waiting for my husband, Ricky, to get home so we could have breakfast. I remember letting out a frustrated sigh when the knock came at the door, angered because I was reading, and things were getting good. I'd bookmarked the page on my Kindle, then threw my fuzzy blanket off and stormed to the door, ready to give someone hell for coming to my house so early on a Sunday.

When I opened the door, my rebuff froze at the sight of a policeman on my front porch.

I crossed my arms, hugging them to myself instinctually in defense, as if I already knew I didn't want to hear what he had to say.

It's funny how everything can be so in focus one minute, and a blur of confusion the next. After he said the word *accident* and *motorcycle*, it was as if he'd morphed into one of those teachers on *Charlie Brown*.

Wa, Wa, Wa Wa Wa Wa . . .

I remember crumbling. Just falling to the floor at the policeman's feet, my entire body numb as my mind tried to make sense out of what the HELL was going on.

Ricky died on impact. The doctors said he didn't feel any pain. He didn't suffer. He was simply there one second, and gone the next. What started as an early-morning ride, ended up changing the course of my life forever.

The ironic thing . . . Ricky had survived four tours in the Middle East, only to be killed on a stupid motorcycle in the good ole US of A, on a deserted street in San Diego, California. I'd lived in terror throughout each deployment, but it had never occurred to me that I'd lose him at home.

PART ONE
The Journey

ONE

"Yes, Mom, I'm sure," I assured her as I tucked the phone in between my ear and my shoulder so I could resume packing.

"I know you think I worry too much, Mirabelle, but driving cross-country all by yourself is crazy." I could hear the strain in my mother's voice, and I understood it, I totally did, but I swear, my mom acted like I was eighteen instead of thirty-two. "Why don't you let me buy you a plane ticket?"

I rolled my eyes, grateful that she couldn't see the insolent act.

"I don't want to fly, that defeats the purpose of this trip," I replied, softening my tone. "I *need* to do this, Mom."

I could feel the fight go out of her, even though she was in Florida and I was in California, it was that palpable.

"Okay, Belle," she said on a sigh. "Just make sure you call me every night."

"I will."

"And, have your car serviced before you leave."

"Done."

"And, make sure you stop every couple hours to stretch."

"Mom . . ."

"And, stop when you're tired."

I laughed into the phone.

"I will. Mom, don't worry, I'll be fine."

"I know," she replied, and I hoped those weren't tears I heard in her voice. "Be safe, Belle. I love you."

"I love you too, Mom. See you soon."

I shut off my phone and stuck it in my back pocket, then looked around the house that had been my home for the last ten years. It was empty now, save the few things I'd kept behind for my trip, and the large open rooms felt as hollow as my heart.

It had been a year since Ricky died, but I'd been unable to think about what to do next, until recently. I'd been comfortable in my grief, and stayed because this is where I felt closest to him.

We'd met twelve years ago in Louisiana, but I moved here once we were married, and the bulk of our relationship was spent here. So when I lost him, the thought of losing San Diego, our house, and our memories, was too much to bear. So I stayed, even though there was nothing for me here any longer.

My parents live in Florida, and I'm an only child.

Ricky's father passed away four years ago, colon cancer, and his mother and sister, Consuela, still live in Louisiana.

I have no family here, and no one that I would call a true friend. I mean, sure, I'd made some friends at work over the years, but with Ricky gone so often, I mostly kept to myself.

He was not only my husband, but also my best friend, and with him gone I'd went from a loner to a hermit.

I'd started drinking. Initially, to ease the pain I'd felt with his death, but lately, I drank because it was four o'clock, and I had nothing else to do. Plus, I liked it. I liked feeling numb. When I drank the anxiety and panic left me. I knew my limits, too. I knew how much I needed to drink to reach that moment of peace, and when I needed to stop before peace became loneliness and grief.

I'd finally come to the realization that I couldn't live this way any longer, so I'd sold the house, had our stuff packed up and loaded on a truck, and was about to embark on my first adventure in years.

I think my mother suspected that I was drinking too much, and I knew she wanted to get me in person so she could confirm her fears, but I wasn't ready to stop. Alcohol had become my friend. The one thing I could rely on to make me feel better, and I wasn't willing to give it up.

Ricky and I loved road trips, and often used them as a way to break out of the mold of our everyday lives. Whenever we took a trip, we vowed to be open to trying new things, and took that vow very seriously.

I was driving cross-country, stopping to see his family, and then my own, before I decided what I wanted to do next with my life. Where I wanted to live. Where I wanted to work.

I was a cook. Not a chef, since I'd never been classically trained, but I'd been cooking since I was old enough to reach the counter in my mother's kitchen. What had started as my mother teaching me what *her* mother had taught her, had turned into a passion, and I'd been working in kitchens since I was sixteen years old.

Over the last few years I'd been working at a diner. Working the early shift and mostly cooking breakfast and prepping lunch, before getting off and having my afternoons and evenings to myself. I wasn't sure exactly where I wanted to go next, but I knew it would be in a kitchen somewhere. I needed at least that one semblance of normalcy in my life.

I took one last look at the shell of what had once been my home, slung my bag over my shoulder, and walked out without looking back.

It was time to move on.

More than Exist is Now Available on all retailers!

About the Author

Award-Winning Author Bethany Lopez began self-publishing in June 2011. She's a lover of all things romance: books, movies, music, and life, and she incorporates that into the books she writes. When she isn't reading or writing, she loves spending time with her husband and children, traveling whenever possible. Some of her favorite things are: Kristen Ashley Books, coffee in the morning, and In N Out burgers.

CONNECT WITH ME:

www.bethanylopezauthor.com

Facebook, Goodreads, Pinterest, Google +, Tumblr, Instagram

Acknowledgements

Allie at Makeready Designs: As always, your cover is gorgeous! Thanks for all the time you've spent helping me with branding and for always listening to my input. I'm so grateful to work with you.

Kristina at Red Road Editing: This has been a busy year for you, but you always manage to find time for me in your schedule. I appreciate the time and effort you put in to helping my work be the best it can be.

Christine at Type A Formatting: I'm so grateful to call you my friend, and to get the chance to utilize your talents. You make my ebooks and print books look so beautiful. I can't wait to see you again!

Jessica at Inkslinger PR: We've had a busy year! Thanks so much for working and growing with me. Here's to killin' it in 2018!

To Ann and Raine for their constant support and feedback. And, Lori, Jennifer, Kristi, and Christine for beta reading and telling me what you think!

To my ARC Team, thanks for being excited with me about these books. For giving me your feedback and for saying, "I can't wait for the next one!"

To my family, for helping me stay dedicated, for understanding how much I love writing, and for supporting me along the way.